CLEANS TO AN END

Squeaky Clean Mysteries, Book 16

CHRISTY BARRITT

River Heights

CHAPTER ONE

"So, Carson hasn't called me back since we went out. Why do I always date the wrong guy, Gabby? Am I cursed? Stupid? Too pretty for my own good?" Clarice Wilkinson paused from scrubbing the floor and looked at me through her hazmat goggles as if I held all the answers.

I *should* hold these kinds of answers. I'd dated every kind of wrong guy before I finally married Riley. I was *so* glad I wasn't in the dating world anymore. So. So. Glad. Like, I'd rather swim through crime-scene sludge than try to find Mr. Right again.

"Listen, this guy is showing his true character," I told her. "That's a good thing. Be glad he's out of your life now instead of after you've invested more in the relationship."

I wiped up some more dried blood from the golden

oak floor of a top-grain house in Norfolk, Virginia. The place was a study in contrasts. Peaceful yellow walls. Freshly waxed floors. And a pool of blood and the subsequent spatter around it.

"My clock is ticking." Clarice's eyes narrowed with over-strung drama. "I want to settle down and have kids."

If she worked as much as she talked, we'd be done with this job a lot faster. But I had a feeling she needed a listening ear, and here I was . . . I might as well use all my bad experiences for good. That's what Jean Valjean from *Les Mis* would have told me to do.

"You're only twenty-three, right?"

"Exactly." Her eyes widened, driving home her point. "I'm getting old. I had all these prospects in college, yet all I wanted was to play the field. Now that I've graduated? All the good ones are gone."

"I'm sorry to hear that?" My voice trailed off into a question.

"You're so lucky you met Riley." Clarice pushed her goggles farther up onto her face and began scrubbing more dried blood from the floor. "When am I going to meet *my* Riley?"

I wished I could answer that for her. But I couldn't. Besides, in my book, Riley was one of a kind.

"Okay, enough about that depressing subject. Do you remember when we first started working together?" Clarice changed topics like Katy Perry changing outfits during a concert. "You used to always play with different jingles. That was so much fun. Let's do it again."

I hadn't tried to come up with a jingle in a long time. But at one point in my life, I'd prided myself in my ability to manipulate lyrics into silly little crime-scene ditties.

"There was one I always thought you should use." Clarice rocked back on her knees—in other words, she stopped working again. "How did it go?"

I shrugged, not sure which one she was referring to. I'd come up with quite a few. Some sounded more like cheers. Some were to the tune of nursery rhymes. I even tried rap a few times and tapped into my Gabby G-Dog persona.

Before I could offer any suggestions, she started singing one of my "Santa Clause Is Coming to Town" remakes. "If you've been shot, if you've been stabbed, if blood on your walls say 'Someone's been bad,' Trauma Care is the-e-re for you."

Wow. It had been a long time since I'd thought about that little song I'd written. "You've got a great memory."

"It would have been a fantastic jingle." She began scrubbing again. "I can totally hear Zooey Deschanel singing it, kind of like she did on *Elf*."

I tried not to snort. "Of course, Trauma Care is no longer the name of the business."

I'd sold my part of the company to Chad Davis,

who'd eventually rebranded. He was now Squeaky Clean Restoration Services.

Clarice shook her head, as if put off by the name change. "So boring. Maybe we can make a jingle for him. Maybe to the tune of 'Twinkle, Twinkle Little Star'? Squeaky Clean is the best. All the others don't pass the test. Cleaning blood is what we do. You should just hope it's not you. Squeaky Clean is the best. And we do our job with zest."

She used jazz hands to pull the whole song together. That, when combined with her hazmat suit, made for a real winner.

"I'm sensing a second career in your future," I told her, not bothering to keep the smile out of my tone.

"I'm sensing sarcasm." Clarice looked up for long enough to shoot me a playful frown. "Let's get back to those jingles a little later. What's going on with you lately?"

I'd forgotten how much my prissy sidekick liked to talk. My prissy *former* sidekick. It *had* been a while since the two of us had caught up.

At times when we were cleaning, it felt like it had been *ages* since I'd done something like this. At other times, I felt like I'd never stopped cleaning up blood, brain matter, and other gruesome aftermaths of death.

I used a scrub brush to get a particularly stubborn bloodstain from the floorboard, glad for my protective equipment. "Grayson Technologies was sold out to a larger company, and they're still restructuring, which basically means they want to keep me close but not too close."

"I see."

"Besides, with everything going on right now, forensic trainings are on hold. Instead of learning how to properly apply fingerprint dust, now all the police departments want to learn about is proper law enforcement etiquette. That's what they're calling it. Etiquette."

"You should write a paper on it. It can be called 'Law Enforcement Etiquette in a Time of Cultural Wokeness and Perpetual Offense.'"

"That title alone would offend people."

"And further drive home your point. Or you could write a song. It could be 'A Soliloquy on Proper Behavior for Crime Fighting in the Key of E Minor.'"

I forgot how funny Clarice could be. She was an entertaining gal. Maybe even a bit like me when I was younger.

Clarice pushed her dirty rags across the floor as we scoured every inch of the room. "Anyway, that's crazy about your job. Things can change in a flash, can't they?"

"Yes, they can." For instance, I never saw myself in this line of work again, not after I'd progressed to bigger and better things. But that was neither here nor there.

"What about your cold cases? I thought that dreamy Garrett Mercer had you busy with that." As she said

Garrett's name, her voice became wispy and her eyes cloudy.

Garrett had that effect on women.

"He does," I told her. "But now that Evie and Sherman are married, they requested a month off. Who am I to deny them the honeymoon of their dreams?"

"Where did they go?"

"New Zealand so they could see Middle Earth."

"Middle Earth?" Clarice glanced at me in confusion. "Is that a band?"

"A band? No."

"An amusement park?"

"What? No. It's a—"

"I know! An archeological expedition!"

"Clarice, Middle Earth is from Tolkien."

She stared at me. "Oh, he's that designer, right? I know someone who has a cute purse like that she bought on eBay . . ."

I resisted the urge to palm my forehead. "Haven't you ever heard of *Lord of the Rings*?"

She twisted her neck as if thinking a little too hard about her answer. "I've heard of that somewhere. It's a movie with those little hobbit people, right? Sounds weird to me."

I shook my head, not even trying to understand her thought process. "What's weird to one person is perfect for someone else."

"Well, while those two are out pretending to be

incredibly short creatures searching for a designer hand-bag, I'm glad you're here with me. Their loss is my gain."

If she wasn't entertaining me so much with her ditzi-ness, I might roll my eyes.

She continued to chatter. "But I'm really sorry that Tommy broke his leg."

Tommy, one of Chad's employees, had fallen from a ladder, and now he was off his feet for at least two months.

It worked out well for me because I was able to fill in and make some cash in the meantime.

Not that Riley and I were hurting for money. Riley was a lawyer, and he was doing fine at his new practice. But I'd never been one to sit at home doing nothing. Besides, it felt good to get back to my roots.

"So what happened here?" Clarice continued, frowning at all the blood we still had left to remove.

"From what I understand, an intruder broke into this woman's home, shot her, and then stole all her money and jewelry."

"I didn't think people did that anymore," Clarice said. "Isn't it so much easier to rip off people's identities or steal their credit card numbers online?"

I wanted to argue, but I couldn't. Her words were so true. "For real. You'd think criminals would know better, right? Now a life has been needlessly lost. All for a measly few hundred dollars."

"I hate to imagine how things played out here."

"I can imagine it a little too well," I told her.

Based on blood evidence, the victim had been standing in the sunroom when the intruder had stepped behind her, taking her by surprise.

He'd shot her once, based on the bullet hole in the wall.

Blood impact from the wound had spattered on the wall.

The victim had fallen to the floor and bled out. Her body had remained there until her family found her the next morning.

The killer had run in the opposite direction, careful not to leave any footprints in the aftermath of the crime.

As always, the crime scene told the story.

One had to just be willing to listen.

Clarice moved to the other side of the sunroom, where the crime had occurred.

This wasn't just any sunroom. It was an exquisite second-story sunroom in a lovely neighborhood.

Windows surrounded us and were filled with leafy green plants that hung and stood and floated, reminding me of a 1950s housewife edition of *Avatar*. A leather couch sat against the wall, and wicker furniture formed a conversation area around it. Not my style, but the place was peaceful and serene.

If it wasn't for the blood.

Clarice and I still had a lot of work to do. Not only

did we have to sanitize this place, but we also needed to check the furniture and the walls for any particulates that we may have missed.

The woman's son had hired us for the job. He couldn't face this himself. Most people whose loved one had been through crimes like this couldn't.

I didn't blame them.

I'd started doing this work after I'd had to drop out of college. I'd always wanted to be involved with crime-scene investigation. When I couldn't do that without my degree, I'd discovered crime-scene cleaning. It was where I'd gotten my feet wet, so to speak. And by "wet," I didn't mean with blood and bodily fluids.

It was just a figure of speech . . . mostly.

"Do you think blood spatter could have gotten in this return vent?" Clarice pointed to the grate on the floor in front of her.

"You should check it, just in case." It always paid to be thorough.

Clarice made a face before pulling it up. As she did, she sprayed some solution inside, took a rag, and began to wipe it out.

"Hey, Gabby." Clarice's voice climbed with what sounded like confusion.

"Yes?" I braced myself for more of her questions. What would it be this time? We'd covered movies, our favorite coffee drinks, her love life, my job, and even jingles.

"I think there's something in here."

My shoulders tightened. "Like what?"

Dust. Let it be a huge ball of dust. I'd even settle for a cockroach or dead mouse at this point.

Based on the catch to her voice, I had a feeling that wasn't what it was.

Clarice reached inside and raised her gloved hand, revealing what she'd found.

It was a gun.

After Clarice showed me what she discovered, I bagged the weapon and then began to pace the room.

Could that gun have been the murder weapon?

I hadn't told the complete truth when I told her I didn't know much about what happened at the house. I'd researched the case before I came. It's what I had *always* done, and I couldn't seem to stop myself.

The victim's name was Regina Black. She was sixty-six years old. She'd retired from banking and had been widowed four years ago. Her husband had worked in finance, and the two of them appeared to be well-off.

I was basing that on the fact that historic homes in this neighborhood went for six hundred thousand and up, as well as my observation that all her furnishings were top of the line.

From what I'd researched online about this crime,

cops hadn't found the murder weapon. They assumed the killer had left with it.

So what about the gun Clarice had found? Was it the murder weapon?

But that wouldn't make any sense. Why would the person responsible shoot this woman and then hide the weapon where it could be found and traced back to him or her?

He wouldn't. It was too risky.

So what if Regina had hidden a weapon in the vent herself? What if she didn't have a gun cabinet and felt like the vent was a safe hiding spot where no one would find it?

I shook my head. What sense did that make?

None.

But that was the problem. No matter which way I looked at this, the whole thing didn't make any sense.

"What are you thinking, Gabby?" Clarice watched me as I paced.

"I'm still sorting out my thoughts, getting them in Do-Re-Mi order." *Do-Re-Mi order*? I wasn't even sure where that came from. Sometimes when I got nervous, weird stuff left my lips without any forewarning.

I thought I'd moved on from that, but obviously I hadn't. Sometimes I just hid it better than others.

"Shouldn't we call the police?" Clarice frowned as if her earlier nonstop talkativeness had been replaced with nonstop anxiety. "What if they missed this?"

"We should probably let somebody know. I mean, it only makes sense."

"You're the professional. You tell me." She narrowed her eyes. "Why do I feel like you're kind of freaking out on me right now?"

I didn't want to tell Clarice the thoughts that brewed in the back of my head. To say them out loud would sound absurd.

Besides, Clarice looked up to me. Like she'd just said, she thought of me as a professional. If I shared my theory with her, she'd lose all respect.

Before I could figure out what to say, Clarice sniffed the air. "Do you smell what I smell?"

"I don't think that's how the song goes—unless you're trying to create a new jingle or something."

"No, not the song. Like, in real life. Do you smell that?"

I took a big whiff also, and, as I did, my stomach sank.

I *did* smell something.

Smoke.

The theory I hadn't dared to voice aloud yet seemed more and more likely.

I sprang into action, knowing we probably didn't have any time to waste. "Let's grab that gun and get out of here. Now."

Her eyes widened. "It's just someone burning leaves, right?"

I shook my head. "The house is on fire."

"How do you know that?"

"Experience." This whole thing strangely mirrored the very first crime scene where I'd found evidence the police had missed. A chill went through me at the thought. "Let's get out of here. Now."

CHAPTER TWO

"You're overthinking this." Chad gave me a hard stare as we stood on the sidewalk while firefighters shot streams of water at what had once been the lovely two-story Victorian home that had belonged to Regina Black.

Clarice and I had climbed out of our hazmat suits and thrown them in the back of the van. Now we waited for this to be over.

Chad—my friend and the owner of the business—had been called and came right out.

He looked tense as he stared at the house, most likely hoping his insurance would handle this, if it came down to it. The easy assumption would be that the fire was started due to something Clarice or I had done.

My friend had recently taken to growing out his beard. He had a thin, lean surfer build and perpetually tanned skin. Chad was a hard worker, and, since becoming a father, he took everything very seriously—sometimes too seriously.

"I *know* my idea sounds crazy." I may have mentioned my little theory to him. "Believe me, I do. But the coincidence between this scene and the scene from five years ago is uncanny. I found the murder weapon there and then the place was set on fire, just like today."

Chad rubbed his chin. "I don't know what to say."

I glanced behind me and saw firefighters saturating the roof to make sure the flames didn't spread. Thankfully, we were able to get downstairs and outside before the fire got to us.

But I was anxious to know the cause of the blaze. I knew one thing—it had been set on purpose. I was certain.

"This is a coincidence," Chad said. "That's all there is to it."

I frowned, wishing I could so easily believe his words. "The very first crime I ever helped solve as a crime-scene cleaner involved me finding a clue the police missed. What happened afterward? The killer set the house on fire."

"But that was so the hidden weapon could be discovered since the police missed it."

"I don't know all the details that happened here today." I crossed my arms, undeterred. "I just know this is weird."

"It does have a little déjà vu going on."

"Yes! Déjà vu makes do-re-mi sense."

"What?"

Before I could explain, a sedan pulled onto the scene. Detective Adams stepped out.

My mouth wanted to drop open, but I held my jaw in place.

As I glanced at Chad, he practically rolled his eyes. "Let me guess—he came to that crime scene too?"

"He worked the case!" I exclaimed. "If Chip Parker shows up, I'll know something is amiss in the universe."

"You're overthinking this."

"We'll see about that."

Detective Adams strode my way. His saggy eyes looked even more saggy than usual, and his steps a little slower. "Gabby St. Claire . . . it's been a while."

I didn't bother to remind him that I was now married with a different last name. "It sure has. Brings back memories, huh?"

"It sure does." His gaze narrowed, almost as if all the respect we'd built for each other over the years was gone, and I was back to being a nosy crime-scene cleaner. "You found something we missed? Is that what I heard?"

"I didn't say that . . . exactly." I had to be careful because some detectives could be awfully sensitive, especially when they were supposed to be such tough guys. Anything that potentially made them seem incompetent could seem threatening. I supposed anyone would have that reaction.

He raised his shaggy eyebrows. "I'd like to take a look at what you found."

"I locked it in my van. Follow me."

We walked across the grassy yard to my work van, unlocked the door, and I picked up the bag I'd placed the gun inside. I handed it to Detective Adams, explaining that Clarice had touched it—but she'd had gloves on. He scribbled notes about everything I said.

"Why does this always happen to you?" he finally asked. He sounded—and looked—as perplexed as I felt.

"I ask myself that same question quite often." For real. I did. I had a knack for inserting myself into these types of situations, sometimes without even trying.

Adams shook his head. "I don't know what to say. I'll be in touch."

"I'll be waiting. But staying uninvolved. Totally uninvolved." If I repeated that to myself enough times, maybe the mantra would stick.

However, that had never worked before.

I couldn't wait to talk to Riley when I got home to the little house we'd bought just over a year ago. The crafts-man-style bungalow had plenty of character and a cheerful disposition with its white siding and picket fence.

I still marveled that this place was mine, while at the same time thanking God for all He'd blessed me with. I truly didn't feel like I deserved the good things in my life, but I was thankful for each of them.

Before finding Riley, I greeted my dog, Sir Watson. I'd found the canine—a German shepherd/basenji mix —as a stray, and we'd been besties ever since. I rubbed the dog's head as he wagged his tail in front of me.

"You'll never believe what happened today." I put my keys on a table near the front door and sauntered across the living room toward Riley.

My handsome husband sat at the kitchen table, chugging a protein shake. He'd obviously just gotten home from the gym—his workout clothes gave it away. He was into parkour, and he'd even been entering some competitions recently. I was just happy that he was happy.

I sat across from him and soaked in his face, one that had become more chiseled and handsome as he'd gotten older. His dark hair was still as thick as it was the day we'd met, but his body was leaner, more sculpted. It didn't matter to me what size he was. I thought he was the best guy around.

"I haven't seen you this excited in a while." He set his shaker bottle on the table and turned his full attention on me. "Please tell."

It sounded so morbid when he said it that way. "Excited is probably the wrong word. But . . ."

I launched into today's events.

Riley tilted his head after I finished, as if trying to find the right words. "That is . . . uncanny."

"*Too* uncanny. Maybe I can excuse finding the weapon. But the fire also?" I stared at him, watching his reaction.

"So, the last time this happened, Barbara O'Connor was responsible. You think she's recreating one of your old crime scenes?"

"No, of course not. She's in jail."

"So you don't think she's the one who killed this woman?"

"No! You're missing the point here."

"Then explain it to me again. You somehow think this crime is directed at you?"

I frowned. I'd wanted more affirmation, more answers, more confirmation. "I didn't say that exactly. But . . ."

"But yes," he finished, a knowing look in his eyes. "That's what you think."

"I don't know what I think. It's just weird."

"I agree with that assessment. What happened today *is* weird."

He was getting all lawyer logical on me. I'd been trying to move to the dark side, where I thought like a no-nonsense attorney. But life was really no fun that way.

"Let's just hope that my next job doesn't involve a dead Elvis impersonator or a crawlspace," I finally said.

That got a smile out of him. "Let's hope."

I drew in a deep breath and decided to change the subject. Maybe he needed more time to process my theory properly. "So, how was your day?"

"I can't complain. Pretty uneventful." He nodded slowly.

Before he could say anything else, someone knocked at the back door. I looked up and saw my best friend, Sierra Davis, with her son, Reef, standing there. She and Chad were temporarily living in a guest house behind our property until they could custom-build their own home at a site about twenty minutes from here.

As Reef waved at me through the glass window of my door, my pulse quickened.

He was a year and a half old and my absolute favorite person in the whole world—after Riley, of course.

I rushed from the table to open the door. Unfortunately, I barely acknowledged my best friend as I swooped her son from her arms.

"How's my best boy?" I turned with Reef in a circle and was rewarded with a toothy smile. He reached toward me, his chubby hand clapping over my cheek as he stared at me.

"Best boy?" Riley asked.

"Well, you're my favorite man, if that's any consolation."

"I'll take what I can get." Riley turned toward my friend. "How are you, Sierra?"

My adorable Asian friend slipped inside, a plate of something in her hands. She was short, thin, and smart —and I wasn't trying to use stereotypes here. That's just who she was.

She'd been a faithful friend to me over the years, and her antics always kept me entertained. She would fight to save hurting animals with her dying breath—and I'd like to think she'd do the same for her friends.

The best way to describe her was as a kitty cat in her personal life but a tiger on the job.

"I heard about what happened on the job site today," Sierra said. "Weird, huh?"

"You can say that again," I muttered.

"Since I was reliving old times, I thought I would bring these by." She sat a plate of something on the table.

I sucked in a breath when I saw the chocolatey cake-like treats. "Are those acorn brownies?"

Sierra shrugged. "I just had the unusual urge to try my old recipe again."

Acorn brownies were exactly as they sounded— brownies made from flour created by grinding up acorns. The treats used to be Sierra's signature dish.

Now that she was married and a working mom, those little cooking experiments had become less and less frequent.

"Is Chad back home?" I knew I should pick up a brownie and try a bite, just as a way of saying thank you for all her hard work.

But as much as I loved the concept of acorn brownies, I didn't *actually* love acorn brownies that much.

Apparently, Riley didn't either because he just stared at them also. Even Sir Watson didn't make any move to steal a treat. And that dog *loved* human food. Of course, we didn't give him chocolate, but that didn't mean he wouldn't try to eat chocolate if he had the opportunity.

"No, Chad's not home yet. He's still at the scene, apparently. The woman's son showed up, and Chad is having to explain to him that none of what happened today was our fault." Sierra plopped down at the table beside Riley. "Why do you think someone set the house on fire with you inside?"

I sat down across from her and settled Reef onto my lap. "That's what I was wondering too."

"I still stand by my earlier statement—maybe you're jumping ahead of yourself," Riley's lawyering tone reared its ugly head again. "Maybe the fire was some type of accident. Maybe there was a heating issue or something."

Sierra and I both stared at him.

He shrugged, a touch of puzzlement in his gaze.

"What? I'm just offering an alternate theory."

"Someone set that house on fire," I stated.

"Does that mean they were inside the house while you were?" Riley asked.

A chill went up my spine. "I don't know. Maybe."

"Well, did you hear anything?" Riley continued.

I almost felt like I was on the interrogation stand. "No, I didn't hear anything. But I may have been distracted by making up rhymes and jingles. We thought that maybe Chad would need a new jingle for his business."

Riley stared at me a moment before letting out a chuckle. "You never fail to entertain me, Gabby—not even after all these years together."

I shrugged again. "What can I say? I consider it my spiritual gift."

It was strange. The past couple of years, since I'd gotten a respectable job where I actually had to dress like a professional, I'd felt so grown up. But now that I wasn't working on a daily basis for Grayson Technologies, part of me felt younger. Lighter. Freer.

It was a strange feeling, but I felt like I'd somehow reversed my aging process.

Part of me liked it.

I knew that the first chance I had a moment alone, I was going to look into the death of Regina Black.

If someone had been trying to get my attention, it had worked.

CHAPTER THREE

REGINA BLACK. SIXTY-SIX. WIDOWED.

I already knew those things, but it didn't hurt to review the facts.

I sat in my bed, darkness around me, and my husband quietly breathing beside me. When I was sure he was sleeping, I'd grabbed my laptop from my nightstand and tried to find answers to the questions that kept me awake.

From all the news reports I'd read about Regina, I'd gathered that the woman was quiet, that she volunteered for a couple of charities, and that she loved gardening.

I still had so many questions.

First of all, her murder was a tragedy. Any time a life was senselessly lost, it was definitely a crime against humanity. But, secondly, had her death really been the result of a senseless home invasion?

I leaned back in bed, my head against the padded headboard, as I tried to contend with my thoughts.

What if this had been a setup? I knew I might be going out on a limb, but I wanted to explore the possibility. What if someone had set up the crime scene today to send some sort of message to me?

It might be a long shot, but I still wanted to flesh my theory out.

If my theory was correct and that was the case, had this person also killed Regina just to get my attention?

That seemed extreme.

Instead, what if this person had heard about Regina's death and then planted the gun?

I frowned. If that were the case, how would whomever had done this know that I was going to be there to clean the crime scene? That was no longer my MO. Besides, a couple of other companies could have been hired to clean up the scene. Where had this guy gotten Chad's name?

When I put all that together, there were so many variables that even I had to doubt that someone had done this to get my attention. Too many unknowns were involved.

I knew I should put this whole thing out of my mind.

I should forget about it. Dismiss today's events as a coincidence.

I was really good at doing things like that. Turning my back on hunches. Pretending like clues didn't exist. Keeping my nose out of other people's business.

Or not.

My mind raced. To make matters worse, I didn't have anything else right now to occupy my thoughts. No other jobs or cold cases or anything.

The closest thing I had to distracting myself was the fact that my father was finally getting married in two weeks. Although I didn't have much to do with his ceremony, I was helping my dad's fiancée, Teddi, with some of the details.

And my brother, Tim, should be finished with his prison sentence soon. Last I'd heard, he had only one month left before he'd be released on parole. He'd started a meth lab at my old place, which had exploded and destroyed the entire apartment building.

I closed my laptop and set it on the nightstand. Then I looked over at Riley as he snoozed in bed beside me.

In the dark, he looked so peaceful. I could hardly tell he'd been the victim of a deranged serial killer only a few years ago. Most of his memory issues had cleared up, and, to meet him, people wouldn't guess the ordeal he'd been through.

That very ordeal had nearly broken me.

That very ordeal *had* broken him.

But the two of us were proof that there was still hope despite tragedy.

I really should focus on those things.

And I would.

Mostly.

But, for now, I sank deeper into my bed, pulled the covers up to my chin, and attempted to turn my brain off so I could sleep.

The next morning, Chad didn't have any jobs lined up for me, and I had nothing else scheduled.

I felt like a lady of leisure as I wandered into The Grounds, my favorite coffeehouse. It was located across the street from my old apartment building.

As I'd pulled up, I'd noticed that another structure was finally starting to be built on that property. Sharon —the tatted, pierced, ever-changing-hair-color coffee-house owner—told me after I'd placed my order that she didn't know what was going up there yet.

I was curious. That space would always hold a very special place in my heart.

After I'd gotten my vanilla latte with extra whipped cream and an extra black coffee, I went back to my car and briefly contemplated what I was going to do next.

And by briefly contemplate, I meant that I knew exactly where I was going.

I headed to the local police station.

Since my early days of working cases, I'd come a long way. I used to be known as a pest to those within the police department. But, thanks to my new job, I was now known as a professional.

I just needed to make sure I kept it that way.

At the front desk, I asked for Detective Adams. I knew he probably wouldn't share any information with me, but it was worth a shot.

A few minutes later, the detective appeared in the doorway. He said nothing, only gave me a quick hand motion indicating I should follow him.

At least, I thought that was what it meant.

Either way, I quickly scurried behind him.

He stepped into his office, and, once I entered, shut the door behind us. I quickly glanced around the space. I'd been here before—on multiple occasions. It mostly looked the same—except I noticed the pictures of him and his wife were gone.

I glanced at his hand.

His wedding ring was also gone.

Maybe that would explain why he looked so worn down.

He let out a deep breath before saying, "I guess I shouldn't be surprised that you showed up here today."

"It has been a while since the two of us have visited with each other." I lowered myself into the seat across from him and handed him a black coffee. Yes, see—there was no contemplation. I'd known from the start how this would play out. "For you."

He raised his eyebrows. "Thank you. But you're not tricking me, Gabby St. Claire. I mean, Gabby Thomas. I don't think I will ever get used to that."

"Sometimes I still haven't gotten used to it."

"What can I do for you?" He leaned back in his chair and stared at me.

I took a quick sip of my coffee before putting on my most affable expression. "I was wondering if you figured out what kind of accelerant was used to start that fire at the house yesterday?"

"I knew it." He wagged a stubby finger at me. "I knew you wouldn't be able to keep your nose out of this investigation."

"Can't a girl be concerned about her community?" I put on an expression of mock offense.

He let out a skeptical, "Uh huh. I'm glad you're here, actually. I have a couple of questions for you."

"Like what?"

"For starters, I wanted to let you know that Regina Black's killer has been arrested."

I straightened. "What?"

He nodded. "It's true. The person responsible is a meth addict who desperately wanted money for another hit. He was arrested after shooting someone else in a robbery attempt. He confessed."

"That's . . . good news." Uncertainty stretched through my voice. Where was he going with this?

"In fact, this guy was being questioned by police at the time of the arson yesterday, so he isn't responsible for that."

"Oh." My shoulders slumped.

"Also, the gun that was found in the HVAC vent? It was reported stolen two weeks ago."

"Good to know." I made mental notes of all these details.

"And one last thing. We found a note inside the barrel."

I sucked in a breath. "What?"

Adams nodded slowly. "It read, 'We've Only Just Begun.'"

"What does that mean?"

"Based on the way it's capped, we're guessing it's from the old song by the Carpenters."

"So, someone left a message." That added an entirely new dimension to this whole mystery. "But why?"

Adams shrugged. "We're looking into it. But, right now, we suspect there are two different crimes going on."

"I see."

"And to answer your original question about what was used to start that fire, we're still waiting for the final results."

"But do you have any hints as to what it might have been?"

Something glimmered in his gaze. "We have hints."

"Is there anything you can share?"

He stared at me for a moment before slowly nodding. "The only reason I'm going to tell you this is because we have a long history and relationship. I know that I can trust you with this information, correct?"

"Of course. You know that I am always at your service if you need it here at the Norfolk Police Department."

He let out another skeptical grunt before saying, "Gasoline."

Gasoline?

I wasn't surprised.

Because that's what had been used to light Michael Cunningham's house on fire also . . . five years ago when this all began.

CHAPTER FOUR

THREE DAYS LATER, NO ONE HAD BEEN CHARGED FOR THE arson of Regina Black's home.

But I was staying out of this investigation.

Really.

I was out like Burr during the election in *Hamilton*. Except, wait . . . that wasn't just a musical. That had happened in real life too.

I wasn't used to my extensive knowledge of musicals creeping into real-life historical events.

Deep.

Just as sunlight filled the horizon, Chad met me in front of my house so we could start today's job. I was helping him with a death scene.

"You ready to work?" Chad asked as we fell into step beside each other.

"I am—as long as there's no mold remediation

involved." I couldn't resist the reference.

"That was the first time we met each other." Chad held his tool belt over his shoulder as we headed toward his work truck.

"That's right. Back when we were rivals."

Chad had come into town—he'd been a mortician— and he'd started a crime-scene cleaning business, closing in on *my* market. Eventually, we'd come to our senses and joined forces. We worked better as a team instead of as competitors.

That very first time we'd met, I'd found the body of an Elvis impersonator in the crawlspace of an old home. We'd been pulled into an investigation on what happened to the man, especially after we'd become targets.

"Those were the days." Chad paused at the back of his truck. "This scene is totally different—no mold or Elvis involved."

"So what is it?" I crossed my arms and leaned against his truck. Just the two of us were working this scene. Clarice had to help her aunt at The Grounds. Apparently, the scene wasn't overly involved and only required a skeleton crew.

"A man who lived alone had a heart attack and died. No one found him for a week—"

I snapped my fingers, realizing this may not involve Elvis but the whole scenario sounded eerily familiar to yet another scene I'd worked.

"I worked a cleanup that sounds similar! The man had been dead so long that his bodily fluids had seeped through his skin and recliner and—"

Chad raised a hand while scrunching his nose. "I know what happened. I even remember the funeral you had for the man. It was hard to forget. And it was one of the first times I realized that you were someone I wouldn't mind being associated with."

"Really? Aw . . . that's so sweet." Chad had never told me that before, and I was all about affirmation. However, what had been wrong with me before that day? I couldn't worry about that.

"All right, enough of this reminiscing." Chad nodded toward the cab of his truck. "Let's get going."

I gave him a salute before climbing in the passenger side.

A rush of nostalgia swept through me as we took off down the road together. Part of me missed these days more than I'd realized.

Who would have ever thought?

I breathed into my respirator, grateful I wore one. Otherwise, the stench in the house would be overpowering.

Though this crime scene wasn't as gruesome as the one I'd mentioned to Chad earlier, it was still enough to make someone with a weak stomach sick.

I wouldn't go into details because they were graphic. Let's just say I was cleaning up fluids that had essentially seeped from a body into the carpet.

The place was an old ranch with peach-colored bricks, dainty iron handrails along the porch, and faded black shutters.

So far, there was really no resemblance in this scene and the scene with the dead Elvis impersonator. That was good news, right?

The other good news was that Chad and I were already wrapping this up after three hours. We'd pulled up the damaged carpet and carried it out to the truck. Chad would dispose of it later at a hazardous waste facility. We also sanitized the room.

Whoever took possession of this house would most likely have it re-carpeted. But it would be clean and safe and cleared of any reminders of death.

There was always that, right?

After Chad and I had taken the last of the carpet out and as the air scrub worked hard to combat the scent of death in the room, Chad pulled his mask up and looked around.

Sweat covered his forehead and cheeks as he drew in a deep breath. "I think we're about done here."

"That's good news."

"And it looks like your theory has been debunked." He sent me a knowing look.

"I guess I can't argue with that." I'd been tempted to

look in the crawlspace for another dead Elvis, but it turned out this place was on a slab. "It looks like I was reading too much into things."

That was a relief . . . and slightly disappointing. Though I shouldn't be disappointed. It was actually good news.

The only thing was . . . that made my hunch wrong. And if my hunch was wrong, I was going to have to stop trusting it. And an investigator who couldn't trust her gut wasn't very useful, in my opinion.

I'd sort all those thoughts out later.

"I'm proud of you," Chad said. "You just admitted you were wrong."

"I've grown. What can I say?" I shrugged, like it wasn't a big deal. Truth was, I hated being wrong like the Wicked Witch of the West hated getting wet.

"You ready to wrap this up?"

I glanced at the room one more time and nodded. "I am."

As I went to grab some of our equipment, something dripped from the ceiling and onto the top of my head.

My back muscles tightened as I glanced up. What was that?

A wet spot had formed there, one that didn't appear very old based on the absence of stains.

"Gabby?" Chad asked.

I nodded above us. "What's that? I didn't notice it before."

Chad followed my gaze. "Maybe they have a water heater up there."

"Maybe." But I wasn't convinced. This was a one-story house, built probably fifty years ago—well before it became popular to put water heaters in the attic.

Chad frowned. "Let me guess—you want to go check it out?"

I shrugged. "I feel like we have a duty to make sure we didn't miss anything. Satisfaction guaranteed, right?"

"That's not really in my contract, but . . . I do like happy customers." Chad's gaze ran along the popcorn ceiling with its brassy fan. "We need to find the attic access."

"I think I saw a ceiling entry in the hallway near the bedrooms."

As we searched for it, anticipation built inside me. Was it a water heater? It very well could be.

My mind shouldn't keep going to worst-case scenarios.

But it did.

What were the odds that the police had missed two important pieces of evidence at two different crime scenes within a one-week period?

I wasn't sure.

Worst-case scenarios were kind of my thing.

Chad pulled down a creaky, attic-access stairway and started up. As he reached the top, he pulled on a string before muttering, "Of course, the light is burned out."

"Use the flashlight on your phone," I called.

A beam flickered on in his hand. "It's a mess up here."

Was it weird that I kind of wanted to see?

"You need me to help?" I called up.

"Can I stop you?"

I shrugged as I hurried after him. Chad had stepped into the attic and started toward the other side of the house, where the drip had come from.

I climbed into the dusty space and sneezed. Chad was right—it *was* a mess up here. Boxes were everywhere. Old furniture. A Christmas tree.

One thing I didn't see? A water heater.

Chad paused in front of me and muttered something beneath his breath.

"Everything okay?" I asked.

"No. We need to call the police."

"Did you find a weapon—something chemical maybe? A smoking gun? A leak caused by a gunshot?" My mind raced.

"No . . ."

"Then what?"

"We have another dead body."

I resisted the urge to ask, "Does he look like Elvis?"

But that was all I could think about.

CHAPTER FIVE

DETECTIVE ADAMS ARRIVED ON THE SCENE TWENTY minutes later.

Chad and I had been careful not to disturb anything. But I did soak in every detail possible for as long as I could.

The dead man appeared to be in his thirties, seemed relatively fit in his athletic pants, and had dark hair. If I had to guess, he'd been dead for a day—long enough for rigor mortis to set in but not long enough for the icky part of the decay process to begin.

Yes, icky. I was a professional, and my terminology obviously reflected that. What could I say?

It looked like he'd died via a gunshot wound to his chest.

Based on the marks cutting through the dust on the floor of the attic, the killer had somehow managed to drag him up the attic steps and place him directly over the dead body of the man downstairs.

That would have been a lot of work. Like *a lot* a lot.

Why would someone go through all that trouble?

There was one other thing that had caught my eye. A message had been written on the man's arm in what appeared to be permanent marker. The words read, "Nothing's Gonna Stop Us Now."

Another song reference.

A song reference that tied these cases together.

It was also the second use of a plural pronoun. Did that mean that there were two people behind this?

Detective Adams shifted as we stood in the kitchen, far away from the opening to the attic. The crime-scene unit had headed up there. I'd called hello to several familiar faces as they went past, resisting the urge to give any unwelcome advice.

"Now, walk me through this again," Adams said

So Chad and I did.

Chad looked annoyed. Time was money when it came to business, and he'd hoped to swing by his house-in-progress to do a few things. This extra dead body was putting a kink in his plans.

An hour later, Adams dismissed us from the scene. I gave one last glance back at the house as we walked away. What had happened inside there?

My guess was that the two dead men weren't connected but that the scenes had been staged that way.

Kind of like what had happened at Regina Black's house.

It was another connection. I had no doubt the same person was involved. The question was, did whoever was behind this think I was going to be there?

There was no way someone could have possibly predicted that.

"It wasn't Elvis," Chad finally said as we headed toward his truck. "I guess you're happy about that."

"No, this still ties in with my crime-scene cleaning history." Even though I felt Chad's eyes on me, I climbed into his truck, ignoring his silent questions.

He quickly climbed in after me and gave me a stare. "What does that mean?"

"You remember Darnell Evans? His body was planted at the scene of that house we were at all those years ago. He was lowered into the crawlspace of the home through the floorboards of the house. This person we just found wasn't in a crawlspace but he *was* in the attic. Don't you see? The killer went up instead of down."

He let out a skeptical grunt. "You're reaching."

I shrugged, dismissing his dismissal. "I think I'm onto something."

"I think you *want* to be onto something."

"Why would I want something like this to happen?" *For real, Chad.* I gave him the look that expressed all my silent thoughts for me.

"Because you love investigating. This is taking you back to your old days. No more stuffy training sessions for you. You like to be in the middle of things. Admit it."

"You don't think I'm good at training officers?" I was prepared to be offended, if necessary.

Chad sighed. "I think you're probably great at it. But that doesn't mean I think it's something you love. I know you. You like getting your hands dirty, not sitting at a desk."

I leaned back in my seat. I wanted to deny his words. But I couldn't. He was absolutely correct.

All this time working my other job, there were moments I'd loved it. But what I really loved was being on the front lines.

Still, I was trying to be a grownup. I was trying to establish a career. And I'd made some great connections within the law enforcement community. I'd become an expert on using crime scene and forensic technology.

But it wasn't the same.

I frowned as Chad and I pulled away from the scene.

But my melancholy didn't mean anything.

Nothing at all.

Because I couldn't follow every whim like Maria in *The Sound of Music*. Even though my life mantra was, when life hands you boring clothes, make hideous outfits out of curtains instead, that didn't mean I'd been given khakis and a white shirt.

But why did staying out of this make me feel so unsettled?

"You really think these crime scenes have been set up to send a message to you?" Riley took a sip of his coffee as he stared at me from across the table at our home that evening.

I nodded. "I know it sounds crazy. But, yes, I do."

He narrowed his eyes in thoughtful consideration before asking, "Why? Why would someone go through all this trouble?"

I swallowed hard. I'd been thinking about that also. And . . . "I have no idea. To send a message?"

"What kind of message? That you should start cleaning crime scenes again?"

"I don't know! But my gut is telling me that something is amiss."

Riley put down his coffee cup—and that's when I knew he meant business.

"Okay, let's say your theory is correct. Who might be behind something like this? Who's so twisted that he would kill in order to send you a message?"

It sounded so ominous when Riley said it like that.

"That's a great question." I rubbed Sir Watson's head as I thought about it. "There are people we can rule out.

People who are in jail, for example. Or others who died because of their own stupidity."

I'd never killed someone. But people had lost their lives while trying to kill me. It seemed like poetic justice, I supposed.

"Let's start with Barbara O'Connor," Riley said.

This seemed like a great place to begin. "Barbara is in jail. If she were released, it would be all over the news, especially since politics were involved."

She'd killed the wife of an up-and-coming senator. The case had been high profile, to say the least.

"Bob Bowling," Riley continued.

"Also in the slammer."

"Tree Matthews."

"I'll follow up, but I'm pretty sure he's locked up and will be for a long time." I paused. "Before we get too far into this, there is one theory we haven't talked about."

"What's that?" Riley narrowed his eyes as he waited for me to continue.

"One of these people we've mentioned who are in jail . . . he or she *could* have an accomplice acting as their hands and feet to the outside world."

He nodded slowly. "True. But we still don't have motive. We need a why."

That seemed easy to me. "Revenge."

"Possibly. But this is a lot of trouble to go through just to send you a message."

I knew that, but I had a feeling the events of the past week went much deeper than just sending me a message.

Someone wanted to toy with me. To play a deadly game in which innocent people were caught in the crosshairs.

But I didn't have enough proof to confirm that yet.

And the only way I was going to know for sure was to wait . . . to wait for more crimes.

I swallowed hard at the thought of it.

CHAPTER SIX

SIERRA BREEZED INTO MY HOUSE THE NEXT AFTERNOON, A frazzled look on her face as she set her purse on the couch and released a long, pent-up breath. But her face brightened as soon as Reef saw her and toddled her way.

"Hey, baby!" She scooped him into her arms.

I stood from the floor where I'd been playing with him. His regular sitter had called out sick today, so I'd filled in. Why not? I wasn't doing anything except pondering my future and two local crimes that had my name all over them.

Besides, I enjoyed spending time with Reef. The boy was a delight.

"How did it go?" Sierra turned toward me. "Did he behave?"

"We made forts and warded off pirates and—"

"No fake crime scenes, right?"

"That only happened once, and I promised never again. Besides, it was just some masking tape and a dead T-Rex and—"

"I remember." She raised her eyebrows and gave me a pointed look.

I studied her a moment, realizing she seemed more stressed than usual. "Did you have a bad day?"

She pushed her glasses up higher on her nose and frowned.

"You could say that." She plopped on my couch.

I stood, wiping any potential dust from my jeans, and sat on the couch near her. "What happened?"

"That's the thing. Nothing happened. But it was still a bad day."

"I'm not following."

Sierra's free hand flung through the air as she began to emphasize each of her points. "When I go to work, I feel like a bad mom. When I stay home from work, I feel like I'm a bad boss. I can't figure out how to do both."

"But you seem to balance it so well." I shrugged. I'd never guessed Sierra struggled with the tug-of-war between family and career.

"Some days, I can ignore the questions and the guilt that taunts me. Other days, I can't. Being a working mom is so hard sometimes." As Reef scrambled from her arms, she buried her face in her hands, the picture of distress.

"I can imagine. I'm sorry, Sierra. What can I do?" My friend didn't usually get this frazzled.

She raised her head, and her gaze met mine. "I'm pregnant."

My eyes widened. "What?"

She nodded, confirming I'd heard correctly. "It's true. I'm due in six months."

"That's great. Congratulations! Are you excited?" I had *not* expected that one.

"I am. But I guess I'm feeling the pressure even more."

"You don't have to do everything, you know." I was, by no means, an expert on parenting or being a working mom. But I hoped I might offer some wisdom anyway.

"I'm doing work that's important to me. How can I give that up?"

"I'm not telling you what to do, but that work will still be there in the future."

"If I don't do it, who will?"

I nibbled on my bottom lip a moment before asking, "Is there anyone else at the office who could help?"

She shrugged. "No one that's me."

"What was it that someone wise once said? You can have it all, but you can't have it all at the same time? I don't have all the answers. But there's nothing wrong with considering your options. Even lionesses take a break from hunting after they've given birth."

"How do you know that?" She stared at me skeptically.

"I was bored yesterday and watched a show on *National Geographic*. Very informative. I learned some other things about lions that I really didn't ever want to know."

She sighed. "I suppose you're right."

Why did she have to sound so reluctant?

"It's just that my pregnancy hormones are making me go crazy." Sierra widened her eyes until I could see the white all around the pupils, and she spread her hands out, trying her best to look insane.

"I can imagine."

She looked at Reef. The boy had found the wooden blocks we'd been playing with earlier and tried to stack them. Sierra's eyes became misty as she watched him.

"I love you, little man," she murmured.

Her son seemed to know something was wrong. He stood, toddled toward her, and leaned forward to give her a toothy kiss. Her entire face lit up again.

"How about if I get you something to drink?" I stood, desperate to do whatever I could to make her feel better. "Some water? Tea? Actually, I'm going to start dinner soon. Why don't you and Chad eat with us?"

"You mean, I wouldn't have to cook?"

"That's right. I'll make some vegan options." I really should have a handy-dandy list of these by now, but I didn't. I should also work more on being the nurturing type. I added those things to my to-do list.

"That actually sounds great, if you don't mind."

"I don't mind at all." I nodded. "You just sit back and relax. I've got this."

Besides, cooking and having friends over seemed like a much safer option than pondering death.

I waited until halfway through dinner before I mentioned the crime scenes.

Everything had been going outstanding so far.

I'd fixed some vegetarian chili using refried beans and lentils instead of meat. I had some frozen rolls I'd been able to bake that were also vegan. Sierra would have to skimp on the butter, but I did put some strawberry preserves out, just in case that sounded like a good alternative. For dessert? Fruit salad.

The meal might not win any awards, but it was rather tasty.

And my friend no longer looked like she wanted to cry, so that was a nice bonus.

I cleared my throat and decided to forgo eating another grape. Instead, I set my fork down and glanced at Chad. "Did you hear from Detective Adams today?"

Chad wiped his mouth with a paper napkin. "No, I

haven't heard a thing. I figured you'd be down at the station asking questions."

I'd thought about it a million trillion times. "I'm trying to use some self-control here. But I have to admit that I can't stop thinking about the body in the attic." I glanced at Reef and lowered my voice—not that he could understand any of this. "Who was he? How did he get there?"

"I don't know the answer to any of those things," Chad said. "But clearly you've still been thinking about this."

"Even if I didn't wonder if there was a connection to my past, I'd still be curious. Both scenes were very interesting and purposefully set up." I thought my points were as valid as my new driver's license from the DMV.

"We'll know something is wrong if Parker shows up," Riley added.

"Those were my exact thoughts!" Whenever Riley and I were of one mind, I had to revel in the moment. It didn't happen often.

Parker was a former boyfriend who now worked for the FBI. He'd started dating a fellow agent, and they'd even had a baby together. They'd since broken up.

I'd really dodged a bullet when the two of us split.

I held my breath, halfway expecting to hear a knock on the door at the mention of the man.

But there was nothing.

"Do we have any jobs lined up for tomorrow?" I asked Chad.

"Nothing. I'll be working on my new place, and I have to replace some doors for an older woman in Chesapeake. Your schedule should be free and clear tomorrow, though."

"You sure you don't want me to listen to the police scanner and go to the scenes to drop off your business card and drum up potential new clients? That was very effective when I was first starting out in the business."

"I think I'll be okay," Chad said. "But thanks . . . I think."

"Clarice and I were working on jingles for your company," I offered. "I could dig into those again."

I began singing our rough draft to the tune of "Twinkle, Twinkle Little Star." "Squeaky Clean is the best. All the others don't pass the test. Cleaning blood is what we do. You should just hope it's not you. Squeaky Clean is the best. And we do our job with zest."

Chad stared at me a minute. "Have you thought about looking for other full-time work?"

I shook my head. "No. Grayson Tech said it's possible I can come back as soon as things sort themselves out."

"There are no cold cases you want to investigate?" Chad continued.

"I *have* been looking through a few cases. But until Evie and Sherman are back, I don't want to dive into anything. Besides, we vowed to only take on four a year. With the two of them working full time and living so far away, it only makes sense."

But I knew what everyone was hinting at.

To use a double negative, I was not good at not doing anything. I needed something to occupy my thoughts.

Otherwise, I might dwell on the fact that, historically, my next case had involved an eco-terrorist bombing.

And Sierra.

I swallowed hard, hoping for once that I was wrong.

Especially now that I knew my friend's news.

CHAPTER SEVEN

"You're going to be the star of the show in this dress." Teddi twirled me around on the little platform where I stood. "You look radiant."

Radiant was right. Why wouldn't I look radiant considering the bright orangish-reddish dress I wore? Even the sleeves screamed nuclear meltdown with their spiked ruffles that shot toward the sky. A bow at the back was also stiff, with points that practically emulated fire.

Definitely radiant.

I was trying on my bridesmaid's dress for my father's wedding, and this was the final fitting.

I suppose I shouldn't be surprised at what Teddi had picked out. She'd always had outlandish taste. The woman reminded me just a tad of Dolly Parton, with her beehive blonde hair, tiny body, and big . . . eyes.

She'd stuck with my father for far longer than I thought she would. Had it really been almost four years? There was a lot to be said for that, especially considering that my dad was a recovering alcoholic. Apparently, he hadn't had a beer in three years.

I hoped he was telling the truth when he said that. He wasn't a nice man when he was inebriated, and I didn't want Teddi to have to deal with that.

"I'm so happy that you are going to be a part of our big day." Teddi clapped her hands as she stared at me.

"I'm honored you asked me to be—although *you'll* be the star of this show, not me."

"You know I think of you as the daughter I never had. This whole ceremony is really about family."

That was really sweet of her. I couldn't say a bad thing about the woman. In fact, she might secretly be a saint.

I averted my gaze from the mirror so that I wouldn't frown as I looked at the dress again. "Is Trace coming into town?"

"He just finished recording his album," Teddi said. "But he should be able to make it."

Her son, Trace Ryan, was just breaking into the country music scene. He was a really nice guy. I'd had the opportunity to meet him out in Oklahoma a couple of years back. I couldn't believe that I was going to have a stepbrother.

"Once we're all done here, what do you say the two

of us go out for a nice meal?" Teddi stared up at me, blinking rapidly, possibly because of her fake eyelashes. She always had trouble with those things.

A nice meal? This wasn't something I was used to Teddi or my father saying.

"I heard Cracker Barrel had a special on their chicken and dumplings," she continued.

I felt a smile. Cracker Barrel? It was a nice restaurant. That just wasn't what came to mind when I'd first heard the invitation. But that was fine.

"I would love to go grab a bite to eat with you," I told her.

See? There were advantages to not working as much. I was getting to catch up on all these things I'd been behind on.

I slipped out of the dress and back into my normal attire. I was becoming accustomed to wearing a more professional wardrobe lately. But today I had donned my favorite skinny jeans and a T-shirt that read "Not Today, Satan." I'd even put on my favorite pair of Sanuk flip-flops, even though it was chilly for September.

"You seem a lot lighter lately," Teddi said as we left the bridal boutique. "More like the girl I knew when your father and I first met."

"Is that right?" Funny that she was the second person to say that.

Had my new job really been aging me that much? Or

was it simply the fact that I had professional responsibilities and had to act the part?

Because buried deep inside me was the same old Gabby. I didn't feel like I'd changed that much. Or maybe getting married made me feel more settled. Now that I wasn't always acting on my insecurities when it came to men, I could focus those energies on other things.

"Anyway, I guess I'm just saying that it's good to see you smiling," Teddi said. "You've always been such a spunky young woman. Working hard in your nine-to-five. Things are finally going your way, aren't they?"

"Well, I do have a lot to smile about. As do you, right?"

"I'm *so* excited to begin this next chapter with your father. I'll tell you what, there are a lot of things in life to look forward to. But love is one of the best."

"It's like an island in the stream, isn't it?"

"What?"

"Never mind. How about if I drive?" I asked as we reached my car. I'd ridden with Teddi a few times, and she seemed to space out at the worst possible moments.

"That sounds great."

Teddi talked on and on about where she and my father were going on their honeymoon. I'd really rather not think about my dad going on a honeymoon at all. But I politely listened.

They planned to head up to the Poconos in Pennsylvania for a week. They'd found one of those old-school-type of cabins with a heart-shaped hot tub.

I'd gone to Pennsylvania not long ago with the Cold Case Squad, and, though the state was beautiful, I still needed some time to recover from everything that had happened during that case. It hadn't been pretty.

My thoughts drifted to my own honeymoon. Riley and I had gone down to Florida, where I'd promptly gotten sunburned and discovered our temporary neighbor had been abducted. The whole thing had definitely been memorable.

As we continued down the road, I saw a plume of smoke rising in the distance.

My stomach tightened.

It was probably nothing. Most likely just the byproduct of one of the industrial areas in town.

It definitely hadn't been an explosion.

No way.

Even if it *were* an explosion, it had nothing to do with me.

This wasn't the third piece of the mysterious puzzle coming together.

My theory had been totally wrong.

But, if that were true, why was I trying so hard to convince myself of that fact?

CHAPTER EIGHT

"Do you mind if we take a rain check on lunch?"

I hadn't wanted the change of plans, yet I couldn't seem to stop myself. I knew that even if Teddi and I went to enjoy some chicken and dumplings together, that my mind would still be on that plume of smoke I'd seen rising in the distance. Until I found out what had happened, I wouldn't be able to stop thinking about it.

That wasn't entirely fair to Teddi.

"Is everything okay?" She looked at me, batting her false-eyelash-lined eyes.

"I just remembered something that I need to do," I told her. "I'm really sorry. But can we reschedule?"

"Of course, of course. Just drop me off at Jolene?"

"Jolene?"

"It's what your father named my car. Since it's red, it seems appropriate, right?"

I wondered if my father and I were more alike than I ever wanted to admit.

I shook my head, putting the thought out of my mind. There was no way that was true—not if I had anything to do with it.

I turned my gaze away from the smoke and made a U-turn. Several minutes later, Teddi was back at her car. I apologized again, waited until she was safely inside her own vehicle, and then I pulled away.

I headed toward the smoke. I had no idea where I was going, but I couldn't lose sight of that anomaly in the sky if I tried.

It *definitely* wasn't a little bonfire in someone's back-yard. The smoke was thick and black. The plume was still going strong.

When I listened, I could hear sirens in the background. The city's finest were no doubt headed toward the scene. If any of them passed me, I suppose I could just follow them. Although it seemed awfully creepy to do things like that.

I'd heard of a case one time where someone was trying to be funny and follow an ambulance, only to have it pull up to their own home. I'd never forgotten that.

I kept traveling through Norfolk, headed toward the waterfront area. The good news was that I wasn't headed toward downtown. That was where the last bomb had gone off, in an office building there. The whole scene had been horrific.

Fifteen minutes later, traffic came to a stop.

I knew what that meant. The road ahead was most likely closed.

I didn't have the patience to wait.

Instead, I pulled into a parking lot, climbed out, and began walking down the sidewalk toward the area ahead. I still had no idea really where I was going, so I just followed the smoke still.

As I walked, I tugged my zip-up sweatshirt closer to my neck. A surprising nip claimed the air today, promising autumn would be here soon.

Finally, I spotted fire trucks in the distance surrounding some type of warehouse.

I walked as close to the scene as I could before an officer stopped me. I stood at the police line and watched as firefighters worked to put out the smoldering flames.

The building was an old aluminum-sided structure located on the river. Based on the crab pots stacked outside, I'd guess the building housed some type of fishing operation.

When I saw "Cityside Seafood" written in faded red letters on an old white truck out front, I knew I was correct.

A car squealed to a stop on the scene. When the driver emerged, I sucked in a breath.

FBI Special Agent Chip Parker had arrived.

That wasn't good news.

Parker pulled down his aviator sunglasses and cast a glance—or was that a scowl?—my way. He then pushed his glasses back up on his nose and strode toward the officials on the scene.

I knew what that meant.

It meant that he'd get back with me later—though whether it would be in a nice or not-so-nice manner was yet to be determined.

I watched as he talked to the officers, and I tried to read his lips but had no luck.

Note to self: *take a lip-reading class.*

I added that to my To-Do List, right under: *learn how to become more nurturing.*

Next, I practiced cultivating the art of patience.

I would *really* love some answers now. In my younger days, I might even have pretended to be a reporter in order to find some of those said answers.

Now, too many people knew me for me to find out information by those means. Instead, I needed to wait. Besides, when I started back up with Grayson Technology, I needed to maintain a reputable reputation. Nobody wanted to learn the latest fingerprinting technology from someone who'd been banned from every crime scene in the area.

The good news was that the flames at the seafood processing plant appeared to be under control.

Had this simply been an industrial fire? The fact Parker was here made me think that it wasn't. The FBI wasn't called in for accidental fires.

A few feet away, two men stood at the crime-scene tape. Both wore coveralls and work boots, making me think they were employed at one of the nearby warehouses. From the way they leaned together and talked while staring at the scene, I figured they were discussing what had happened.

I decided to use my time wisely and approached them. "Excuse me, do you know what happened here?"

"We were working in the next building over when we heard an explosion," the taller, lankier man of the two said. "We hustled out here after it happened and haven't heard anything."

"Do you know if there were any combustible materials inside?"

Mr. Lanky stared at me for a minute. "I'd ask if you are a reporter, but you certainly don't look like a reporter."

I glanced down at the snarky T-shirt that peeked out from under my sweatshirt. This was the moment when I'd find out if wearing my casual outfit would help me or hurt me. I had a theory on this . . .

"I'm not a reporter," I told him. "Just a concerned citizen."

He didn't even bat an eye at my statement. "As far as I know, there are no combustible materials inside. It's a seafood-processing plant. Makes this whole area smell terrible."

"Were there people inside?" Honestly, that should have been my first question.

But my gut told me that there wasn't anyone inside. Otherwise, the ambulances would have been busy taking people to the hospital. I hadn't seen any of that, which was surprising.

"Nobody works here on Saturdays," the man said. "It's a good thing because this place employs about a hundred fifty people. If this had happened yesterday, this would be a whole different scene."

I repressed a shudder. "You're right. It would have been."

I crossed my arms as I continued to watch.

An hour later, Parker finally strode toward me.

I held my breath as I waited for what he had to say . . . and I hoped he might share some details.

CHAPTER NINE

"FANCY SEEING YOU HERE." PARKER TUCKED HIS HANDS into his pockets in that casual manner he was known for.

When I'd first met him, I couldn't help but think that he looked just like Brad Pitt. I'd quickly learned that Parker didn't fit my mental description of what I thought Brad Pitt would be like. The man was brash, selfish, and pretty much nothing I really admired.

Since I first met him, he'd aged, like we all had. He was still handsome, but his lifestyle seemed to be catching up with him. More wrinkles had appeared around his eyes and mouth. His hairline was starting to recede. He had smoker's lips. And he'd probably gained about twenty pounds.

Aging happened to the best of us, I supposed. Even beautiful people.

"I saw the smoke on the horizon and decided to see what was going on," I finally explained.

He gave me a smoldering stare. "Is that right? You know what they say about curiosity and cats."

"That the two of them go together like peanut butter and jelly?"

"No, that's not what the saying is."

I knew that, but I wouldn't give him the satisfaction. Instead, I changed the subject. "So, any chance you'll tell me what happened here?"

He grimaced as he looked back at the building. "You know I can't do that."

"It must be something big if you were called. I know you can't say what but . . ." My statement trailed, begging him to fill in the rest.

He ignored me. "What are you really doing here, Gabby?"

"I heard there was a big explosion. Since there weren't any combustible elements inside, that leads me to believe that it could have been a bomb."

His gaze flickered before he said, "No comment."

I let out a *hmmph*.

"Let's try this for the third time. Why are you really here, Gabby?"

There was no use living in denial any longer. "Because I think someone is recreating some of the crimes that I've solved . . . and, if this scene is what I think it is, I'm afraid I'm right."

"Are you serious, Gabby?" Parker stared at me as if I'd just told him the NSA had admitted aliens were real.

I didn't want to nod, but I did anyway. "As serious as a dead man at his funeral."

"Why would someone want to recreate any of the crimes you've solved?"

I shrugged. "I've been asking myself that question also, and, the truth is, I don't really know."

His facial muscles tightened again. "I don't like the sound of any of this."

"Don't worry, neither do I. The good news is Sierra doesn't have any connection with this place."

As soon as the words left my lips, realization washed over me.

This was a seafood-processing plant.

This was *exactly* the kind of place Sierra—an animal rights activist—hated.

She very well could have some type of affiliation with this place.

What was I thinking?

I needed to talk to her. Now.

"I should probably go." I took a step back, desperate to get back to my car and warn my friend.

Parker's gaze narrowed. "You're not fooling me. What are you thinking?"

"I'm not thinking anything. You know me. I don't

like thinking." Of course, Parker knew me well enough to know that I more than liked to think about everything. I liked to overthink. "I just need to check out something."

"Is it anything I should know about?"

"No." I didn't sound convincing, only overly dramatic.

"This is a serious matter, Gabby."

I repressed a shiver. "Believe me, I know."

"If there's anything you discover that I should know about, you have my contact info."

"I will let you know," I told him. "I promise. Because if my hunch is right, this isn't something that I'm going to want to face alone."

I said that because I knew what was coming if my theory was correct.

And what was coming was absolutely unthinkable.

CHAPTER TEN

Sierra had told me earlier that she was going into work for a few hours this morning, even though it was Saturday.

With that thought in mind, I headed to the office building for Paws and Furballs. The one-story hexagon-shaped structure had weird angles inside, almost like the architect hadn't been able to make up his mind how to design the space so he'd done a little bit of everything.

I hadn't been here in ages.

I walked inside, but nobody sat behind the reception desk to greet me—that task was reserved for the overwhelming scent of incense instead.

My gaze wandered to the back of the building, where I saw Sierra standing behind a glass partition. I charged toward her.

She looked up in surprise as I walked into her office. "Gabby. I wasn't expecting to see you here."

"I have a question for you, Sierra." I got right to the point.

She froze from sorting papers with "Fight for Fins" across the top. That must be her newest campaign.

Fins? I swallowed hard. This wasn't good. I could only assume she wasn't talking about people from Finland.

"You might want to sit down." I worried about my friend, especially knowing she was pregnant.

I didn't want to bring any undue stress on her.

But I couldn't avoid asking this question either.

It was especially important because, if I was right, I needed to talk to her before the police made any type of connection between that bombing and my friend. But mostly, I prayed this was all a mistake. That I was over-reacting. That my theory held absolutely no merit.

Basically, I was praying that I was wrong—not something I often did.

Slowly, Sierra lowered herself into the chair behind her desk, just as I'd asked. "You're scaring me. Is Reef okay? Chad?"

"Oh, yes," I told her. "They're fine. This isn't about them."

Her shoulders visibly softened. "I'm glad to hear that, at least."

I sat across from her, trying to temper my words so I

didn't upset her any more than necessary. "Sierra, have you ever been to Cityside Seafood?"

Please say no. Please say no. Please say no.

"Cityside?" She perked. "That's funny that you brought them up."

I held my breath as I anticipated what she might be about to say.

"I actually went there this morning. How did you know?"

My stomach sank. Then clinched. Then nausea pooled in my gut. All kinds of digestive issues happened all at once, which was never a good sign.

"Oh, Sierra . . ." I rubbed the side of my head, where a subtle pounding had already started.

She squinted. "Okay, you're scaring me again."

"Why did you go to Cityside?"

"They have inhumane processing practices for their seafood. Did you know they asphyxiate their fish on ice before processing them? People don't think that fish have feelings, but I'm here to tell you that creatures with fins matter too. They may not be cute and furry, but they deserve to be protected. Do you know what else they do at the place? They take the fish and—"

I raised my hand. I really didn't want to hear this. I liked eating fish too much.

"Let's skip that part," I said. "What did you do when you stopped by the facility?"

"I told them that they needed to change their

processes and made it clear that we would ask nicely first but, if they didn't comply, we had other not-as-nice ways to stop them."

I squeezed the skin between my eyes, wishing it was some type of button that would extinguish my urge to throw up. Her words *could* sound like a threat.

"When I said ways to stop them, I meant the campaigns we'd start against them, which would give them bad press. Not anything violent."

I still couldn't bring myself to say anything. *I* knew that, but would other people?

"Gabby, what's going on?" Sierra leaned closer, studying me in confusion. "Why do you look so devastated? I have conversations like this with companies all the time. It's no biggie."

"Sierra . . . somebody just set off a bomb in that building."

She blinked as if she hadn't heard me correctly. "A bomb?"

I nodded. "I had that crazy theory that someone was recreating some of the crimes I've solved. Now it looks like I'm right . . . because the last time a bomb went off, you were framed for it."

My friend's face lost all its color. She didn't argue with my assessment.

Because she couldn't.

My words were true.

Now Sierra was in the crosshairs.

How was I going to fix this?

I had called an emergency meeting at my place. Sierra put Reef down for a nap in my bedroom, so the timing worked out well.

Riley, Chad, Sierra, and I all sat in my living room, tense expressions on each of our faces.

"Obviously, Sierra didn't do this." Chad's voice sounded tense, and his muscles looked tight.

"I know that," I said. "But the question is, what are the police going to think when they realize she was at Cityside Seafood this morning?"

Chad shook his head before raking a hand through his hair. "I can't believe this."

Riley put on his attorney persona, looking at ease as he took on the role of even-keeled mediator of the group. "What did you carry inside with you when you went, Sierra?"

"Just my purse." Sierra's face looked more stoic than usual.

"That's good news," Riley said. "Because a bomb of this magnitude wouldn't fit in your purse. The police will try to figure out how somebody got an explosive into that building and when. What did you do after you left?"

"I climbed in my car and went back to the office."

Sierra froze, and her face went pale again. "Actually . . ."

"What are you thinking?" Chad's gaze latched onto hers as he watched her every move and listened to her every word.

"I went back because I realized I hadn't left my business card," Sierra said. "When I went back inside, the owner—Mr. Forrester—wasn't in his office."

My stomach clenched even tighter. "So then what happened?"

"So then . . . I wandered into the processing plant area to see if I could find him." Her breathing seemed more shallow as she paused. "I still didn't see Mr. Forrester, so I don't know where he went. Maybe he stepped out back."

"What did you do next?" Riley asked.

"I went back to his office, left my card, and then I went to my car."

Chad frowned. "Did anybody see you?"

"There was a homeless man on the sidewalk. I suppose if he was paying attention then he would have seen me."

This was getting worse and worse. If Parker managed to track down that homeless man, and that guy told the FBI he'd seen Sierra go back into that building, she'd definitely be their number one suspect.

Today's events couldn't have played out any worse.

The same question still lingered in my head. How was I going to fix this?

At this point, I had no good ideas.

As I pondered the thought, a knock sounded at the door.

Instantly, my muscles tensed faster than a cheetah chasing its prey.

My gaze shot around the room, and I saw that each of my friends had the same question in their eyes.

Was this the police coming to arrest Sierra?

I peered out the window, but I didn't see any police cars out front.

That had to be a good sign.

"We have to answer it," Riley said.

As I glanced at Sierra, I saw Chad squeeze her hand. My friend leaned into her husband.

I so desperately wanted to protect her. I wanted to tell Sierra to hide. That I'd lie and inform anybody who came to the door that she wasn't here and that I had no idea where she'd gone.

But both Chad's and Sierra's vehicles were outside. There would be no way to keep up a façade for long, especially not with Reef.

After a moment of hesitation, I opened my door.

To my surprise, no one was there.

Instead, a package rested on the welcome mat, my name crudely written in black letters across the front.

There was no address.

No postage.

Someone had dropped off the six-by-six-inch box for me.

All kinds of alarm bells went off in my head as more memories filled me.

CHAPTER ELEVEN

I CHARGED OUTSIDE AND SCANNED THE STREET.

Whoever had left this package was long gone.

The bad feeling in my gut continued to brew. It didn't brew like coffee. No, the feeling brewed like an evil witch whipping up a stinky concoction before she cast a deadly spell.

"What is it?" Riley appeared behind me.

I pointed to the package, nearly unable to speak, which wasn't common for me.

His eyes widened when he saw the box. "That's not good."

No, it wasn't. In the past—while working another crime—I'd received a bomb in the mail.

Was that what this was? If I touched the package, would it explode? Or if I leaned closer to smell it, would I notice an almond scent?

I had so many questions.

I knew the best way to handle this would be by calling the police.

But if I called the police, they'd show up at my door and they might think about questioning Sierra.

I crossed my arms over my chest, unsure exactly what I should do.

Sierra and Chad appeared in the doorway also, and their gazes went to the package at my feet.

"Oh no," Sierra muttered. The wispiness in her voice made it sound like she might be on the verge of passing out.

My friend remembered also. I didn't have to spell my theory out.

Chad put an arm around her waist and led her back to the couch.

Maybe I should clear her out of this house. Send her back to the guest cottage out back, just in case.

I didn't know.

And that was probably exactly what this man had been anticipating. He'd laid out an intricate web. Now I felt stuck in that very web, knowing that whatever decision I made, I was going to continue to be trapped.

That wasn't going to work for me.

I might be stuck for now, but I *would* be coming up with a solution. Soon.

However, right now, I had to figure out if this was a bomb or not.

As we slipped back inside the house, separating ourselves from the package, Chad turned to Sierra.

"Maybe you should go on a trip," Chad said. "You should go on some type of private personal retreat where you don't even tell me where you're going and you leave your phone at home. If you leave now, you could be gone before the police realize any of this has happened."

Sierra pushed her glasses up on her nose and shook her head, a certain heaviness surrounding her. "I'll only be running from the inevitable."

"Maybe by the time the police find you, the real killer will have been apprehended," Chad continued. "So then they won't even need to find you at all."

Sierra frowned. "If I run, I'm going to look guilty."

Sierra had a point. But I was on Chad's side right now. I wanted her to leave. To get out of harm's way.

Riley stepped closer. "If you don't run, then what will you do?"

I glanced back at the package on the porch. I'd left the door open so I could keep an eye on it. Either way, I couldn't get it out of my mind, despite the conversation around me. I only hoped it wasn't literally a ticking time bomb. Riley had insisted that I leave it there and not touch it.

Sierra raised her chin as she faced all of us. "Maybe I need to go to the police myself."

"That's a terrible idea." Chad shook his head back and forth, the action making it clear where he stood with the issue. "Absolutely terrible."

"I don't know," Riley said. "I know this isn't what you want to hear, but maybe it should be a consideration."

"We could always make up an alibi for you." Everyone turned to stare at me. I let out a weak laugh when I realized what I'd just said. "Just kidding. Of course."

Sierra frowned before jutting her non-existent hip out and staring us down. "You guys, listen to us. We're adults. We're no longer a ragtag team of misfits trying to find our way in this world. I have a child now who's depending on me. I can't act like a juvenile."

Her words seemed to sober all of us, and a collective heaviness hung in the room.

"We just want to protect you," I finally told her.

"And I appreciate it," Sierra said. "I really do. But I need to be responsible here."

I let out a long breath, knowing she wouldn't change her mind and that her choice was the right one. I couldn't be in denial any longer. "If you're going to call someone, at least call Parker. Ask him to come over here so we can explain things to him. He knows us. Maybe he'll even have a little compassion."

Slowly, we all nodded.

I glanced at that package again and wondered exactly what was inside.

The one thing I knew for sure: the next couple of hours were going to be life-changing in more than one way.

CHAPTER TWELVE

PARKER ARRIVED THIRTY MINUTES LATER. HE STOOD ON THE porch for several minutes and stared at the package. Then he slipped on some gloves, reached down, and lifted the box.

I held my breath and braced myself for fire and explosions.

Nothing happened.

Instead, Parker shook it, looking more like a kid at Christmas than a special agent. "It's too light to be a bomb. I don't hear any ticking noises. I don't smell almonds."

Maybe he had a point but . . . "Maybe it's not a bomb, but what if it's . . . anthrax?"

He wasn't taking this seriously, was he?

Parker cocked an eyebrow and stared at me as I stood on the grass a good six feet away from him. "You really think that somebody would go to extreme measures like that? Do you know how hard it is to get anthrax? Besides, they could just put that in an envelope."

"I've never actually looked into it. Well, maybe I did once, but that's an entirely different story and doesn't pertain to this at all. But you have to admit, this package is suspicious. It wasn't mailed to me. Someone personally dropped this off."

"I agree." Parker slowly nodded. "I'm going to test it for fingerprints, just in case. There's a chance that one of your neighbors left this for you and there are cookies inside. You know that, right?"

I glanced back at Sierra. We hadn't told Parker *everything* yet. But he was about to find out about my friend's connection to Cityside Seafood. Then maybe Parker would understand exactly where I was coming from.

Sierra stepped closer, her features looking drawn and her skin pallid. Thankfully, Reef was still sleeping so he didn't have to experience any of this.

"I need to talk to you, Parker," Sierra started. "It's important."

Parker straightened, his back seeming to stiffen at her words. "What's going on?"

"Can we all sit at the table?" Sierra nodded toward the dining room.

"Of course." He brought the package inside and set it on the floor, obviously not concerned about it.

I supposed he'd dust for fingerprints later. I was dying to know what exactly was inside that package, however. At least, I could find some comfort in the fact that Parker didn't seem worried about it.

Answers were going to have to wait.

As soon as everybody sat at the dining room table, a cry came from the back of the house.

Reef was awake.

I stood, feeling an overwhelming need to protect the boy. "I'll get him."

I hurried to the back bedroom and scooped Reef into my arms. In his sleepy state, he rested his head up against my chest, nestling it there.

I held the boy tight and prayed he would never know what it was like to grow up without a mother.

I'd lost my own mother when I was in college. I was thankful to have had her all throughout my childhood, of course. Kids should have mothers. *Reef* should have Sierra.

My stomach sank again as vomit roiled inside me.

Not now. Not now.

I snuggled Reef as I moseyed back down the hallway. I joined the gang just in time to hear Sierra wrapping up her story.

Parker had taken some notes and made all the appropriate grunts and nods as he listened.

I held my breath as I waited to hear what would happen next. Would he arrest her? Did he believe her?

I knew Parker, but sometimes the man surprised me. Still, I preferred that he be here rather than some stranger. With a stranger, I didn't know what I was getting.

Parker remained quiet a moment before shaking his head and letting out a small sigh. "I have to admit, this doesn't look great."

"I didn't do this." Though Sierra appeared calm on the outside, her voice climbed a few octaves.

Parker turned to her. "The good news is there's not enough evidence to arrest you solely based on the fact you were there. But there *will* be an investigation. We'll need to look to see if you bought any bomb-making supplies. We'll search your web history. We'll even talk to your coworkers."

Sierra nodded. "I'm okay with that. I don't have anything to hide."

"I appreciate you coming to me with this information."

Parker glanced back at me, and I saw the questions in his eyes. He was probably thinking about our earlier conversation where I said these crimes could tie in with me.

Instead of saying anything, Parker nodded at the package, which now sat just inside my front door. "Now, let's dust this baby for fingerprints and see what's inside."

I held my breath as I watched Parker carefully unfold the brown paper around the box.

He'd set it on my dining room table, and we'd all stood around him as he'd dusted the outside for prints.

There were none, which didn't surprise me.

No doubt Parker would take this back to the field office and experts there would check for any trace fibers. I knew all about stuff like that and all the equipment the forensic technicians would be using.

But I was even more curious right now about what was inside this box.

Sierra had taken Reef from my arms, and she now held her son close.

Meanwhile, Riley stood beside me, an arm casually around my waist.

The tension in the room was so thick, it was like it had gained the freshmen fifteen and then some in a matter of three seconds flat.

Once the inner box was revealed—it was just a plain brown cardboard box—Parker also dusted that for prints. There were still none.

Again, that wasn't surprising.

I almost felt like I was watching someone open a Christmas gift. Only my feelings weren't nearly as warm and fuzzy.

Parker began to slip the top of the box off.

I could hardly breathe as I waited to see what was inside. Would it be something ghastly? Maybe a finger, like in the movies?

Or would it be something more abstract? Like a poisoned apple?

Or would this be a total letdown? Had my dad or Teddi spontaneously left me a gift, without a thought as to how it might be received?

I still had no idea.

But I had a feeling if someone I knew had left this, there would be fingerprints on the outside.

Parker grunted as he peered inside.

I looked over his shoulder, trying to get a glimpse of the box's contents.

But before I could, Parker lifted a paper from inside.

Paper? Someone had gone through all this trouble just to wrap a piece of paper?

Words were slashed in heavy black ink on the crisp white sheet.

Slowly, I read the message that had been left there.

Gabby, as the Backstreet Boys might say, maybe we should Quit Playing Games.

My hand went to my stomach.

It was just like I feared.

This was all about me. No more confirmation was needed.

CHAPTER THIRTEEN

WHILE PARKER DISAPPEARED INTO THE KITCHEN TO MAKE A phone call, I looked up at Sierra. She bounced Reef in her arms, that worried expression still on her face.

I hoped she didn't hate me. I knew she probably didn't, but I wouldn't blame her if she did.

As Riley and Chad talked in quiet tones in the corner, I stepped closer to my friend.

"This is all my fault," I murmured. "I am so sorry."

She tilted her head, the same compassion she held for animals showing in her gaze for me now. "Gabby, you're not responsible for any of this."

"All of this mayhem and destruction is directed at me. Now you might be caught in the crossfire." My voice cracked as I held back emotions. "If something happens to you because of me, I'll never forgive myself."

"Nothing is going to happen to me," Sierra said.

Chad stepped forward. "I'll make sure of that."

"I think the best thing that we can do right now is to try and figure out who might be behind this," Riley said, ever the voice of reason.

"I've already rattled off some suspects." I pulled my haggard gaze up to meet Riley's. "Nobody actually seems likely."

"We need to go through them again. We need to follow up. Now that we know these events aren't coincidences but are targeting you, we need to really nail down some suspects."

I nodded. I liked that idea. "Let's go ahead and make a list. With Parker's help, maybe we can thin out all the names of people who dislike me."

Parker wandered back into the room, slipping his phone back into his pocket. "I can get Sierra's statement here," he announced. "But we're going to need your computer."

"That's fine," Sierra said.

"I'm also going to take this box to the field office so we can investigate it for any clues," Parker said. "Doesn't seem like we're going to find anything, but we want to be thorough."

"Of course," I told him.

Parker made no move to leave. "We're going to need a list of possible suspects from you, Gabby. I need to know whom you've made mad."

"My only problem is that the list is so long. I hardly know where to start." When I said it that way, I felt like the most hated woman in this area. Considering that most of those who hated me were criminals, I supposed that wasn't a terrible thing.

"Write everybody down, and we'll go through them one by one. We don't have any other choice at this point. It sounds like this guy's behavior may continue to escalate."

Escalate? I didn't like the sound of that. "Of course. I'll do whatever I have to do to make sure whoever is behind this is found."

Parker locked his gaze with mine, suddenly seeming all business. "Then let's get started."

Three hours later, everybody was gone except Riley and me.

But the somberness still remained in the air.

I'd made a list of thirty people. Yes, thirty people. Many of whom were in jail now.

Parker was going to look into those individuals. He had access to the correspondence each of them had with the outside. So if someone I'd implicated in a crime was incarcerated, Parker could possibly discover if the person doing this had an accomplice.

I didn't know.

None of us did. None of us except the perp behind these crimes.

I was glad Parker was helping. Some things I simply couldn't do.

But that didn't stop the rumble of nerves from sweeping through me.

Riley pulled me into a long hug as we stood there in our living room. I buried myself in his arms.

"It's going to be okay," he murmured.

I shook my head. "How can you even say that?"

"What do you mean?" He stepped back just enough to look me in the eye.

"If this guy continues to follow this pattern, then you know what's coming, don't you?" My voice cracked as I said the words.

Riley didn't say anything, but I knew that he knew. I could see it in his eyes.

There was absolutely no way I could spell this out. Not right now. Not if I wanted to keep my sanity.

"We'll catch him before that," Riley said.

"What if we don't?"

"You can't think like that," he told me.

"But Riley—"

"I know."

He squeezed my arms, and I saw a flash of fear in his eyes. The emotion wasn't something I saw very often.

"I know," he repeated, his gaze steady.

How could either of us forget? Forget that a maniac

had walked into Riley's office one day and shot him in the head. We hadn't been sure then that Riley was going to make it.

Thankfully, he had.

But our whole relationship had changed. I hadn't been sure if I was ever going to get him back. And Riley wasn't sure if he was ever going to get back on his feet.

The incident—the tragedy—had been one of the most trying times of my whole life.

Now that possibility loomed on the horizon again.

I couldn't even bear the thought of it.

I couldn't bear the thought of losing Riley again.

I wrapped my arms around his waist.

I didn't want to ever let my husband go.

But there was one thing he had right.

We absolutely had to catch this guy before that crime was recreated.

We had no other choice.

At that thought, I reached up and planted a firm kiss on his lips.

"What was that for?" A smile curled his lips.

"Because I love you."

"I love you too." He stooped down, and his lips captured mine again in a deep, lasting kiss.

CHAPTER FOURTEEN

RILEY AND I WENT TO CHURCH THE NEXT MORNING. OUR congregation met in a local high school and was led by the ever-faithful Pastor Shaggy. His real name was Randy Macintosh, but I liked my nickname better.

I tried to stay focused during the worship service, but my mind kept wandering back to everything that had happened. My distraction must have been noticeable because several people stopped and offered to pray for me afterward.

I let them. You could never have too much prayer in your life. Prayer and caffeine, in that order.

As soon as the service ended and Riley and I had climbed back into his car, my phone rang. It was Parker.

My breath hitched. I hoped he had an update for me.

Quickly, I put the phone on speaker so Riley could hear also. "Anything?"

"Good morning to you too." Parker's tone sounded as dry as ever. "And as a matter of fact, yes, I do have something."

"I can't stand the suspense. What did you find out?" I swallowed hard while I waited.

"I'll get to our suspects in a moment. There's something else that I think you'll find even more interesting. There were actually some clues in that box."

I must not have heard him correctly. "There was nothing but a paper inside."

"That's how it seemed, isn't it? But it turns out that the ink that was used to write on the note is made from a beauty berry."

"A beauty berry?" Had he made that up? I'd never heard of such.

"That's correct. There's one place around here where these are found."

"Where is that?"

"The Dismal Swamp."

I swallowed the lump in my throat and pushed memories of that place out of my mind for now. "I see."

"The berry usually has a magenta-colored juice. But whoever used it for this letter dyed the liquid with a darker synthetic ink."

"Sounds like he went through a lot of trouble."

"That's not all. The paper used to write that note is the same kind of paper we found at Milton Jones's old place. He ordered it from Germany and told someone once that he liked the feel of it better than ordinary paper."

The hollow feeling in my stomach became even more hollow.

"Are you sure it's not just standard paper?" I clarified. "Paper that anybody could have gotten?"

"Maybe. But you don't want to rule out this as a possibility," Parker said. "Unfortunately, I'm not done yet. There was one final clue."

Part of me didn't want to know, yet I had to know. "What's that?"

"A single hair was left in the bottom of the box."

"What kind of hair?"

"Blonde. Relatively short."

When I heard blonde, I'd thought of Clarice. But she had long hair. Was that significant?

"Short as if it came from a boy?" I clarified.

"Based on the length, it could go either way. We have it out at the lab right now, seeing if we can do any tests on it. But even if we do find some type of DNA, there's no guarantee that the DNA will be in our system. However, it may offer some indicators as to who it came from."

I didn't think we had enough time to wait for those results, not if my gut was correct. "This person . . . do you think he's trying to send us a clue as to what's going to happen next? Who his next victim might be?"

"I would say that's a good guess."

"He meant it when he said quit playing games, didn't he? This guy is giving me clues, and he's getting serious."

"That's how it appears. I'm sorry, Gabby."

"Me too."

As I ended the call, I turned to Riley. Only one thing was on my mind. But if I said it out loud, I was going to sound crazy.

I prepared myself for a *choo-choo* . . . because I knew the crazy train was about to come into the station.

"It's Milton Jones," I announced.

My words hung in the air.

Riley turned fully toward me, his gaze dead set on mine. "Gabby, you saw Milton Jones die with your own eyes. There's no way it could be Milton."

"He's the only one who makes sense." That's when I began ticking off reasons on my fingers. "He taunted me. Took me to the Dismal Swamp. Left me threats. It *has* to be him."

"There's no way he could have survived what happened."

That moment flashed back into my memory. The moment where Milton and I had a confrontation in the woods after the man had held me captive.

I'd thought for sure he was going to kill me.

I'd managed to escape, but he'd hunted me down. It was dark and storming all around us. The swamp had practically come to life, rising like Sandman to become a force all its own.

The raging wind had caused a tree to fall over and crush Milton.

His death had effectively saved my life.

"Gabby?"

My mind snapped from the memories and back to the present.

I looked at Riley, trying to focus. "Yes?"

"You know there's no way Milton could be alive."

"What if he wasn't the one who died?" I knew my words sounded outlandish, but I needed to explore every possibility here.

"He confronted you in the woods. He chased you. Who else could it have been? Besides, the police took his body. Don't you think they checked it?"

"Maybe. I . . . I don't know. But he was clever. Maybe he could have—"

"I think you're jumping ahead of yourself here, Gabby. I know you want to find this guy. But you need to consider the idea that it's somebody else who's using Milton Jones's methods to confuse you. If it was Milton Jones, do you really think that he'd make it that obvious?"

I shivered. "I guess not. But Milton was undeniably

the most evil man I ever went face-to-face with. That's why he makes the most sense."

"He's dead. It's not even like he can be corresponding with someone right now and setting these events into motion."

I nodded, knowing I didn't have any good counter-argument. There wasn't one.

"We still have other suspects that we can look at," Riley said. "Let's not get tunnel vision and just focus on Milton, okay?"

I nodded again, even though I felt numb.

"Milton had a son, didn't he?" Riley asked.

"He did. But his son died of cancer last year." I may or may not have occasionally done research on him.

"I'm sorry to hear that."

There was one more thing that I couldn't stop thinking about—one more clue that could possibly lead us to answers. "Whose hair was in the box?"

"Who do we know with relatively short blond hair?"

I quickly searched my thoughts, faces flashing through my mind. I wouldn't call Chad's hair blond anymore. It was getting darker all the time now that he wasn't surfing as much as he used to. Sierra had dark hair. Riley had dark hair. I had red hair. Clarice had long blonde hair.

I could keep going through this all day, trying to run through people I might know who fit.

I only knew that if this guy continued his pattern,

that the next case I'd solved involved an old friend of Riley's who'd disappeared. Even though it ultimately turned out that there was more to the story, Riley's friend had still died.

Part of me felt like I needed to send out an SOS to anybody who knew me, telling them that they needed to be careful until this passed. But how exactly did I do that?

I didn't know.

But I needed to carefully plan my next steps.

Because the people I cared about . . . their lives depended on it.

CHAPTER FIFTEEN

AFTER RILEY AND I DISCUSSED THE CASE, I CALLED SIERRA and Chad to see if they wanted to have lunch with us. Sierra told me that she and Chad wanted to have a quiet time at their house together instead.

Part of me felt like the two of them were huddling down, anticipating the fact that Sierra might be hauled to jail at any time now.

Guilt again pressed on me at that thought.

Guilt would get me nowhere right now. Finding answers would.

First, Riley and I grabbed something to eat at our favorite Mexican restaurant. Afterward, we headed to The Grounds to grab some coffee.

When I walked in, I spotted Clarice working behind the counter.

I paused near her and leaned into an oversized

pastry display as Taylor Swift crooned "Look What You Made Me Do" overhead.

"Where's your aunt?" I asked.

"She took the day off," Clarice said as she frothed some cream, a slightly frazzled look on her face.

"It's unlike her to take time off."

"I know." Clarice raised her voice to be heard over the machine. "I've been on her for a while about letting me help her more. I'm glad she finally listened. I was thrilled when I got the text from her this morning asking me to fill in. Plus, I could use a little extra cash."

That sounded like a win-win.

Sharon was a fixture around here, a therapist to those who were coffeeholics. I always enjoyed talking to her, and she'd even let me stay in the overhead apartment a couple of times when I'd needed a place to go.

Riley and I ordered. A few minutes later, our drinks were in hand and we found a table in the corner.

I wished this was just a lighthearted discussion about our future or our favorite TV shows. But Riley and I both knew it wasn't.

Riley set his non-froufrou coffee down. "Let's talk about what we know one more time."

"Let's start with our suspect list."

"First, there's Barbara O'Connor," Riley started. "She's in jail and, according to Parker, she hasn't had any visitors in three years."

Parker had offered up that information last night in a surprising loose-lipped moment.

"Okay, so it seems she can be ruled out."

"Next is Bob Bowling," Riley continued. "He's also in jail. But he didn't strike me as the type who would do something like this. He wasn't the smartest criminal that we've ever encountered. And, really, his motive was financial."

Bob had killed Elvis. Okay, he'd killed a fake Elvis. An Elvis *impersonator*. "I agree. I can't see him being responsible for this."

"That would bring us to Tree Matthews." Riley twisted his neck in doubt. "But Tree was really a criminal with a mission. He never had a vendetta against you per se."

"I can't see him being responsible for this either. And that brings us to the crime we solved while at your reunion at Allendale Acres in the mountains of Virginia."

Riley nodded slowly. "That's when my friend Jackie Herrington disappeared."

"But it turns out the person responsible for everything was the hotel manager, Bentley. But, really, he wasn't a violent man. He was just trying to cover up his auto theft ring."

Riley let out a sigh. "Of everyone we've been through so far, I feel like we can safely rule out the people we just mentioned."

"I agree," I said. Most of them had been oppor-
tunistic criminals, not the types who liked to intricately
plan revenge or murder. "And that brings us to Milton
Jones."

Riley and I stared at each other for a moment. I knew
what he was thinking. He was thinking that Milton was
the most likely suspect.

Riley and Milton went back. Way back. Riley had
been the prosecutor during his trial in California, a trial
that ended with the man being put away for life. But
while being transferred between prisons, Milton had
managed to escape and had immediately come after
Riley.

"He could've faked his death," I reminded Riley.

"I still stand behind my reasoning it would be
impossible for him to fake his death based on the
circumstances of how he died. Plus, the police examined
his body."

I wanted to argue with him, but I couldn't. It didn't
really matter which way I looked at what had
happened, it would have been nearly impossible for
Milton to switch places with somebody right before that
tree fell. I had to use common sense here.

"Do I need to go on?" I asked.

"Let's stop there for a moment," Riley said. "I think I
have enough people to think about. I don't want to
muddy up my thoughts too much."

"I agree." I took a sip of my drink and let all those

faces of the people who hated me swirl in my head for a moment.

I wished solving a murder was like spinning a giant wheel and whatever name the dial stopped on was the killer.

If only it were that easy.

By the time I took the last sip of my coffee, my thoughts were still swirling. Each of my earlier cases replayed in my mind, in all their glorious and not so glorious moments.

I'd put other people in jail also. A lot of other people. Eventually, I'd try to rule them out too.

But I was bothered by the fact that Milton Jones kept rising to the surface like a body dumped in a lake that just wouldn't sink.

Riley was clearly right. The man was dead. I needed to wrap my mind around that and mark Milton off as a possible suspect. There was no way he was behind this or that he'd trained someone else to be behind this.

So why was he the only one who seemed to fit?

I kept looking at my phone, waiting for another message from Parker. For an update.

But there had been nothing.

The good news was that Sierra hadn't called yet to tell me that she'd been arrested either.

What a mess all of this was.

As I took another sip of my drink, I glanced at Clarice and frowned. She was the only one working right now, and she had a fairly long line. I'd worked here on occasion while in between jobs several years back. Part of me wondered if I should jump in to help her now.

I loved Clarice, but she was a little scatterbrained sometimes. At least, she wasn't as petty as she'd been at one time. She'd grown a lot over the last several years.

As I contemplated if I wanted to jump in to help, my phone buzzed with a text.

"Is it Parker?" Riley asked.

I hoped that also. But when I glanced at the screen, a number I didn't recognize appeared.

I clicked on the message and saw a photo pop up.

My stomach clenched when I saw it was a picture of a woman's face. Actually, just one-fourth of her face. An eye.

A blue eye that had been crossed out with an X.

Just like the photos Milton Jones used to send.

CHAPTER SIXTEEN

"DO YOU RECOGNIZE THE PHOTO?" RILEY SCOOTED HIS chair over so he could see my phone better.

I shook my head, unable to get the image out of my mind. "It's only one-fourth of a face. It's really hard to tell much by it. Plus, it's a little blurry. But this is clearly a message, Riley. Whoever's doing this wants to let me know that their next victim has been chosen. It's probably somebody I know."

Riley frowned but didn't argue. "You're probably right. We need to send this information to Parker."

My hands trembled as I attempted to hit a button on my phone.

Before I could, I saw that whoever had sent that picture was texting something else. Three little dots appeared, and I waited to see what he was typing.

A moment later, his message came in.

Play the Game, Gabby St. Claire.

I glanced at Riley. "He's using my maiden name. Is that significant?"

"I wouldn't rule anything out right now."

"This is a Queen song."

"It is."

"The only Queen song worth referencing is 'Bohemian Rhapsody.' Doesn't he know that?"

Riley gave me a look, and I realized this was no time to discuss music. This guy was clearly trying to send a message.

"Should I respond?" I asked, my fingers poised on my keypad.

"I wouldn't. Don't give him that satisfaction."

Riley was right. If I engaged with this man, I might end up encouraging the psycho to keep doing this.

Just as the thought went through my head, the hair on my neck rose.

I glanced around.

What if this person was watching me right now? What if he was getting a kick out of seeing my reaction?

"What is it?" Riley leaned closer.

"I have that strange feeling that this guy is close."

Riley scanned everything around us. But he didn't see anyone either.

Then again, windows lined the front of the building. Numerous people hurried along the busy sidewalk outside. Buildings stood across the street, and cars were parked along the curb.

Someone could be lurking in any of those places.

Someone who wanted to watch.

Who got a sick satisfaction out of seeing people scared.

"Call Parker," Riley told me. "Now."

Riley and I talked to Parker, and then forwarded the text message and picture to him. He told us to hold tight, and that he and his team were working on things. They didn't have any leads yet but were putting a lot of resources into finding this guy.

The conversation hadn't been entirely helpful.

But I had a feeling that Parker didn't know any more than we did.

Out of curiosity, I called Detective Adams. I knew he probably wouldn't share any information with me, but I figured talking to him was worth a shot. I also figured it was better than sitting here not knowing what to do.

To my surprise, Adams answered on the first ring. "Gabby, I was wondering when you would call."

"I know it's none of my business, but I wondered if you had any updates on that man who was found in the attic?"

"We've identified his body. His name was Tony

Patagonia. He was thirty-six, and he owned a shoe store in Norfolk."

None of that rang any bells.

"Did he have any kind of criminal history?" Riley asked.

"None. Upstanding guy. Single. Family in the area. He went out for a jog five days ago and never returned home."

"You have no idea who's responsible for killing him?"

"Not yet. But we're working diligently. We've also been in contact with the FBI. I understand that my cases might be in some way connected with that bombing in Norfolk yesterday."

"Seems like that's a possibility," I told him.

"Things are always interesting when you're around, Gabby St. Claire."

He'd just used my maiden name. Just like the person who had texted me. Was that a coincidence?

My heart beat faster.

Detective Adams knew about all my cases. He'd followed along with almost every one. Sure, he didn't really know about the one in the mountains. But he could have easily found out information on that through law enforcement networks.

There was one more thing.

Music.

Whoever was behind this knew I loved music. That I

loved quoting songs. Doing musical renditions when no one was looking.

Not many people knew that about me. Only those who were close.

My blood felt a little cooler.

I shook my head. I didn't like where my thoughts were going. I liked Detective Adams. I didn't want to see him as somebody who might be responsible for this.

"Gabby? Are you still there?"

"I'm here." I snapped back to reality.

"We're working on this case. Hopefully we'll have some answers soon. In the meantime, if there's anything else we need to know, please don't hesitate to give me a call."

As I ended that call, I glanced back at Clarice again to see if she had the line under control. I'd totally forgotten about the fact that I'd been thinking about helping her. The text message had distracted me.

The line had gone down, but Clarice was looking at her phone and a knot had formed between her eyes.

I excused myself from Riley and made my way toward her. "Are you okay?"

"I'm feeling like I need to have some help here. I tried to call Aunt Sharon to see if there was another employee who could come in to give me a hand, but she's not answering."

"What do you mean? Sharon always answers."

Clarice looked up and nodded. "You're right, she always does. That's why I'm getting frustrated."

I remembered the picture that had been sent to me. The photo of someone's blue eye.

Then I remembered Sharon.

She had blue eyes.

And her hair was currently blonde.

My throat tightened.

It couldn't be . . . but what if it was?

CHAPTER SEVENTEEN

RILEY AND I CONVINCED CLARICE TO CALL THE COPS. Adams and Parker agreed to meet us at Sharon's place. Clarice then closed The Grounds so she could go with us to her aunt's place.

Maybe we were overreacting. But I couldn't risk it.

If something had happened to Sharon, we couldn't compromise the crime scene.

When the three of us pulled up to Sharon's small house, her beat-up Ford Fiesta was still out front. We arrived before the detectives—she just lived down the street from the coffeehouse—and I pounded on the door to see if she would answer.

She didn't.

She'd just moved to this place a year ago. Before that, she'd lived above The Grounds for years. When Clarice moved in with her to save money, Sharon realized they needed more space than what the small apartment offered.

Clarice started to pull out her keys and go inside, but I put my hand over her arm.

"Riley and I should go in first," I told her quietly.

Her eyes widened as my words registered with her. "You think Aunt Sharon could be inside? Hurt?"

I opened my mouth to answer but, before I could, two cop cars pulled onto the scene.

Right on time.

Clarice frowned, her eyes containing a wariness that only panic and fear could bring. I'd seen it enough times before. I'd experienced it myself.

After a brief exchange, one of the cops took Clarice's keys and went inside.

I rubbed Clarice's back as we waited for the police to emerge with an update.

"What if they find her . . . dead?" Clarice's chin quivered before she burst into tears.

I pulled her toward me and let her cry on my shoulder. Riley lingered a few feet away—close enough to be there for us but far enough to give us some privacy.

Please, Lord, let Sharon be okay. Bring comfort to Clarice. Bring this guy to justice.

I muttered the same prayer over and over again.

Finally, Detective Adams pulled up.

I kept thinking about my earlier realization about the

man. He *did* have a connection to these cases. He knew about the details.

Could he secretly be some type of mastermind criminal?

As I stared at his droopy jowls and sleepy eyes, I had a hard time picturing it. I had a feeling he was doing well to get out of bed and get dressed each morning. He always looked tired, but he looked especially tired lately.

"Anything?" Adams asked as he started toward us.

I shook my head. "No one answered, but Sharon's car is here."

"Let me go check with my guys."

That sounded like a good plan.

Because there was one other reason that we shouldn't go inside. One besides not disturbing the evidence.

If something had happened to Sharon, I didn't want Clarice to stumble upon her. Cleaning other people's crime scenes was one thing. But it was an entirely different story when you saw someone you cared about as a part of a crime scene. I didn't want to put Clarice through that. Not if I could help it.

She continued to cry on my shoulder.

I could hardly breathe as we waited. I really hoped that this was some type of misunderstanding.

Then again, all along I'd been hoping that this was some type of misunderstanding, and it hadn't been.

But there was still hope that this time would be different. Maybe Sharon was doing something totally out of character. Maybe she had taken off on a trip. Maybe she'd gone shopping. Maybe she was at the spa, and she'd locked her cell phone in a locker.

I really couldn't see Sharon doing any of those things, but I still held on to my fragile hope.

Finally, Detective Adams emerged from the house. I tried to read his expression, but it was nearly impossible.

He paused in front of us. "She's not inside."

My stomach sank, along with my hope. On the other hand, I was thankful her body hadn't been found inside. "Did anything offer a clue as to where she might be?"

He shook his head, a grim expression on his face as if he also thought something was amiss. "I'm going to run that photo you sent me against a photo of Sharon and see if they match."

"The photo?" Clarice looked from Adams to me.

My stomach clenched. I hadn't told her about it.

I braced myself to share the news with her.

When I did, she let out a sob and buried her face deeper into my shoulder.

Riley, Clarice, and I all reconvened back at The Grounds while a crime-scene crew searched Sharon's place.

Rain had started to fall outside, which had precipitated our move to this location. We couldn't go inside Sharon's house for fear we might disturb any unseen clues.

Adams, Parker, and a couple of other law enforcement professionals met with us. We kept the door locked so no customers could enter.

Clarice was still beside herself, to say the least. Her eyes looked dazed and her motions almost robotic. She'd handed out coffee to everyone, probably just to keep her thoughts occupied.

I really felt badly for her. But the best thing I could do to help her was to focus my efforts on finding clues that would help locate Sharon.

We all sat at a table in the middle of the room, our coffees turning cold in front of us.

"Let's go over this again." Parker leaned forward with his elbows on the oak table. "When was the last time you saw your aunt?"

"I saw her last night right before dinner." Clarice's voice trembled. "I got dressed and then headed out to hang with my friends. She swung by the house for a few minutes before heading back to work for the evening."

"Did she say if she had any plans afterward?" Parker asked.

Clarice shook her head. "Sharon hardly ever has plans. She's pretty much a homebody when she's not working."

Adams tapped his pen on the table. "So she wasn't dating anyone?"

Clarice practically snorted. "No, definitely not. Sharon loves being single. Ever since her divorce, she's had no interest in dating."

"And she doesn't have any friends that she likes to hang out with?" Parker clarified.

"She considers everybody who comes into the coffeehouse her friend," Clarice said. "I guess she really doesn't have any other friends outside of that."

My heart panged in my chest. When Clarice said it that way, guilt filled me. I considered Sharon a friend. But maybe I should have checked on her more or asked her to hang out.

Or was what Clarice said true? Did Sharon just like being alone when she wasn't working?

I should know the answer to that question, but I didn't.

"You said she worked here last night?" I clarified.

Clarice nodded. "That's what she told me."

"You do have security cameras here, right?" I asked. "I seem to remember Sharon putting them in after everything that happened with Milton Jones."

Milton Jones had affected all of our lives, hadn't he? He'd bonded Clarice and I forever when we'd both been abducted.

"The monitor where we can watch the footage is in

the back," Clarice said quietly. "If you think it will help, I can show you."

"I'll go look," Parker volunteered.

"Do you mind if I go with you?" I asked. "I'm in here a lot, so I might see something that you might miss."

That was true. But Parker had also hit on Clarice before, so I thought it was best if the two of them didn't spend too much time alone. Clarice did *not* need any Parker drama in her life right now. Been there, done that, and I had the T-shirt to prove it.

Parker stared at me before finally shrugging. "Sure. I guess."

I followed him to the back of the building.

Part of me hoped we'd see something in one of those videos that would give a clue. The other part of me prayed I wouldn't see anything horrific.

Mostly, I just wanted this nightmare to be over.

CHAPTER EIGHTEEN

"You always manage to find yourself knee-deep in things, don't you?" Parker muttered as we stared at the tiny monitor in front of us.

Clarice had shown us the equipment and then disappeared back into the dining area. It was just as well. The space was small, appearing to be an old closet located beside the walk-in fridge.

The only good news was that it smelled like cinnamon and chestnuts.

"I don't like this any more than anyone else does." I tried to stay in my own area and avoid an accidental knee brush as Parker and I sat side by side. It was hard in the tight space. "People I care about are in the line of fire. That's not okay."

His shoulders seemed to soften. "You're right. I didn't mean to imply otherwise."

He continued to scroll through some footage. As he did, I studied the screen, looking for anything that seemed out of place.

"So, Grayson Tech was bought out," he said.

I supposed this was as good a time as any to talk about that. "That's right. I guess no one can resist a good paycheck, huh? With police departments refocusing their energies on more 'woke' methods of training, forensic instruction has been put on hold for now."

"To be honest, I never really thought that career was right for you. Don't get me wrong. I thought it was great that you were doing something on a professional level. And I'm sure you've made some great contacts."

I shrugged, trying not to read too much into anything he said. "The job has been good for me. It's given me some flexibility with my schedule so I can still do other things, and you're right, I have made a lot of good contacts."

He cast a quick glance my way before continuing to study the video footage. "You ever thought about going to work as a crime-scene tech for the police department?"

"I thought about it. I guess I just need to figure some things out, don't I?"

"Figuring things out is always good. I wish I could do that sometimes." He sounded melancholy as he said the words.

I had to wonder what was going on in his life. Since

we'd lost touch, I didn't even have any good guesses. "How's George?"

"She's growing up fast but doing great. I think Charlie and I have finally figured out this whole co-parenting thing."

Charlie was his ex-girlfriend and baby mama.

Just then, something on the screen caught my eye. I sucked in a breath as I pointed. "Is it just me, or has Sharon been talking to that guy for a while?"

I leaned closer, trying to get a better look. The time stamp read ten thirty. I knew Sharon usually closed up by eleven.

"It doesn't necessarily mean anything," Parker said.

"I know it doesn't. But I also think it would be foolish to dismiss this."

"Agreed."

I kept an eye on the time. The man stood there and talked to Sharon for at least twenty minutes. I tried to get a good look at him, but it was impossible. He wore a dark baseball hat and a heavy jacket. Plus, he never lifted his face to the camera.

Almost as if he knew it was there.

Not only that, but it was hard to get a feel for how old he was or how he moved.

It was almost like he knew someone might see this one day and all his actions were purposefully subdued.

My spine stiffened.

Was I looking at an image of the person behind these crimes?

Because if I was then this man was calm, cool, and collected.

Those were horrible traits when it came to a killer.

A few of Clarice's friends came by the coffeehouse to keep her company.

Parker and Adams stood to the side and compared notes on a few things. They'd told me that they were going to talk to some of Sharon's neighbors to see if any of them had seen anything. They would try to ping Sharon's cell phone and look at security cameras in the surrounding area.

While they did that, Riley and I sat at a corner table. We had already gone through everything we'd learned today. But now there was something else I wanted to talk about.

I pulled a notepad and pen from my purse. Yes, I carried one wherever I went. Sometimes, it just helped for me to write things out freehand and to sort my thoughts that way.

Right now was nothing different.

"What are you thinking?" Riley looked like the perfect mix of tired and concerned. But his gaze was also steadfast, and I knew he wasn't anywhere close to giving up on this.

"I still think that these crimes might have some type of tie to Milton Jones. Yes, he's most likely dead. I can't see how he wouldn't be dead right now. But that doesn't mean that there's not some type of connection with his case and these crimes."

"So what are you thinking?"

"I want to jot down every person we can think of that we encountered while investigating his case."

He shrugged. "It seems like a long shot, but I suppose it can't hurt."

"Great." I raised my pen. "I figured the most logical person to start with would be Rose Turvington."

Rose had been my landlord, but she'd secretly been in love with Milton Jones. However, she was in jail now.

"There's always Rose," Riley said. "But that was clearly a man in that video."

Parker had let Riley take a look at the security footage also.

"It's true, but that doesn't mean that Rose isn't helping somebody else again, just like she did last time." She'd been Milton's right-hand woman and had mindlessly helped him in any way she could.

"What about Colin Belkin?" Riley asked.

Colin was a friend of Clarice's. When all the craziness with Milton Jones had been going on, he'd devised a plan to plant false clues at crime scenes and then record my reaction to finding them. He'd hoped to get picked up as a reality show.

"He was just involved because he wanted to become famous."

"But he was connected with Clarice," Riley reminded me.

I shook my head, trying to recall what Clarice had recently said about him. "I have a hard time seeing it. Last I heard, he became an accountant and got married."

Riley sighed. "I have a hard time seeing it too. But I'm just throwing everyone I can think of out there. There are also members of The Guardians."

The Guardians were a notorious street gang in the area. I'd had run-ins with them in the past also.

Who *hadn't* I had a run-in with?

"It could be one of them," I told him reluctantly. "T-Bone. Ice Man. But they weren't the most intelligent criminals I've ever met. They're a more creative type of guys than planners, you know?"

"I get that."

I glanced over at Parker and Adams and frowned. The two of them appeared to be comparing notes at a table across the room.

"What are you thinking?" Riley lowered his voice and leaned closer. "I can see your wheels turning."

I couldn't possibly voice my theory out loud. Yet I knew I needed to talk it through, no matter how bad it sounded.

Still, I hesitated before finally saying, "Both Adams and Parker were involved in those cases. They know all these details. They know me."

Riley's eyebrows shot up, and he lowered his voice before saying, "You think that one of them might be involved?"

I shrugged, trying to subdue my emotions and not give anything away in case someone glanced over at us. "I don't want to think that. But they're both smart enough to pull something like this off. They're involved enough to know things that only the killer knows."

Riley slowly swiveled his head back and forth before glancing at Adams and Parker across the room. "I don't know, Gabby . . ."

"I'm not pointing fingers or making accusations. I'm just brainstorming. I'd be foolish if I didn't at least *consider* them as possible suspects."

Riley glanced over at the two men again and frowned. "You're right. I just don't like the idea of that theory being correct. Those are the guys we're supposed to be able to depend on."

"I don't like the idea of it either."

"What would their motive be?"

"When I went to Adams's office, I saw he'd taken down all the pictures of his wife. He's not wearing a ring either. Maybe he's getting a divorce and the trauma of it triggered something in him."

Riley practically cringed. "I don't know. People get

divorced all the time, and they don't end up as serial killers."

He had a point. But there were certain markers that profilers looked for . . .

"Then there's Parker." I glanced at him. "He's narcissistic, he used to talk about his dad pushing him around as a kid, and he has a hard time forming close relationships."

"I'm still not convinced."

I let out a breath. "Okay, fine. I get it. I really do. I'm just saying we should just keep our eyes open."

"Yes, we should. In the meantime, let's keep that theory between the two of us."

"Good idea."

My phone buzzed, and I looked down at it.

I had gotten another photo.

With a touch of trepidation, I clicked on it so I could see what an unknown person had sent.

It was a photo of Riley and me. At the coffee shop earlier. Beneath it were the words, "I Love the Dead."

The breath left my lungs. When I'd felt like someone had been watching me earlier, I'd been right.

The killer had been close.

Close enough to get a photo of Riley and me.

Just who was this guy?

CHAPTER NINETEEN

THERE WAS NO WAY I COULD REST, AND I KNEW IT.

That man was taunting us.

"I Love the Dead" was an old Alice Cooper song. This guy was clearly sending messages to me. He wanted me to feel fear and dread.

It was working.

But aside from my own anxiety, I also worried about my friends. Sharon was missing. Sierra could be blamed for a crime she didn't commit.

That's why Riley and I headed out to talk to someone named Freddy Mansfield when we left the coffeehouse.

We'd met Freddy while investigating the case against Milton Jones. Freddy was somewhat of an expert on serial killers and all things macabre.

I hadn't seen the man in a couple of years, and I

didn't look forward to seeing him again. But maybe he would know something about an obscure follower of Milton Jones that we hadn't heard about.

He'd recently released a book about serial killers that was doing fairly well. Riley even thought he'd seen the man on one of those investigative shows on TV, speaking as an expert witness about an old case.

We arrived at Freddy's place, climbed from the car, and paused for a moment on the sidewalk out front. Since I last talked to Freddy, his accommodations had been upgraded—however, they looked the same, only bigger. His new house—like his old one—appeared like it could be straight from a scary movie.

Fitting for someone like Freddy.

The white house with peeling paint was an old Victorian with two turrets, skeletal trees out front, and a large, semi-inviting porch. And by semi-inviting, I meant inviting like opening a first page to a horror novel.

When I rang the doorbell, something that sounded like ghosts flurrying through old hallways filled the air.

I shivered.

No doubt, Freddy had intended that reaction when he'd set up his system.

"This guy's a creep," Riley muttered. "I still remember meeting him the first time. He's . . . unforgettable."

"He's an unforgettable creep, but maybe he's an unforgettable creep who could know something."

"I guess we'll find out." Just as Riley muttered the words, the front door creaked open. Of course, there *had* to be a creak involved.

A sliver of a pale face appeared, examining us skeptically from the shadows.

"Hi, Freddy." My voice sounded as dry as the history that stretched between the two of us.

He pulled the door open farther as who I was registered with him. "Gabby St. Claire?"

I wasn't sure if it was a good thing or not that he remembered my name—including my old last name. What was up with people forgetting I was now Gabby Thomas?

As he stepped into the sunlight, I got a better look at him. The man was nearing thirty, had thick dark hair, and the beginnings of a pouchy stomach.

He glanced at Riley and nodded formally. "Long time no see."

"Hey, Freddy," Riley muttered.

"What brings the two of you by here?" He leaned in the doorway and grinned, as if seeing us had made his day.

"We were wondering if we could have a word with you," I started.

"I would be honored." He straightened and

stretched his arm behind him with a flourish. "Be my guest."

Riley and I glanced at each other before stepping inside.

I hoped this didn't end up being a hauntingly royal waste of time.

Freddy leaned back in his leather recliner and thrust his slipper-clad feet out onto the matching ottoman. Did I mention he was also wearing a velvet robe and a tweed flat cap?

The man was definitely a character. If he pulled out a cigar, then he'd totally fit the stereotype I had of him in my mind.

Thankfully, he didn't.

His walls showcased pictures of Alfred Hitchcock along with collectable weapons. A fake coffin served as a coffee table. Candelabras decorated the mantel.

"All this is very interesting," Freddy said after we gave him a basic rundown on what was going on. "But I'm not sure why you're here talking to me."

Riley and I glanced at each other before I dove in. "The truth is that I'm wondering if this has something to do with Milton Jones."

Freddy's eyebrows shot up. "You think he survived what happened?"

I shook my head, resigning myself to the fact that the man had died. I'd seen it with my own eyes. The police had collected his body. I needed to stop even considering that possibility if I wanted to retain any kind of credibility.

"No, I think Milton died that day," I said. "But I wonder if somebody who follows Milton Jones is somehow upset with me for an act he or she thinks equates to me killing him. Now, I wonder if this person is seeking revenge."

Freddy nodded slowly and tapped his chin with his index finger. "Very interesting. This was not a conversation I ever foresaw myself having."

"I know you've done extensive research into all the serial killers of the past few decades. In all of your research, have you come across anybody who has offered to take up the torch for Milton?"

Something flashed in his eyes. Freddy pressed his lips together as if he didn't want to speak. That wasn't going to work.

"Freddy . . ." Riley's voice held warning.

Riley was more intimidating now that he'd been working out. He'd always been athletic, but his office job had started to show. He was now trim and fit and tougher than ever.

"I don't know." Freddy's voice wavered.

"Obviously, you remember something," I said.

The man had a terrible poker face.

"I don't want to throw anybody under the bus." He frowned.

"Is this person your friend?" I asked, trying to read between the lines.

"My friend?" His expression looked aghast. "Of course not."

"Then why does it matter? Someone's life is on the line," I reminded him. "This is no time to be polite."

He raised his palms as if surrendering. "Okay, okay. I just didn't want to jump the gun on anything. I'm a researcher, not a fighter." He paused as if another thought had captured him. "Is there anything in this for me if I'm right?"

Riley bristled beside me, and I squeezed his forearm before he said anything he might regret later.

"If there's anything that I'm allowed to share about this case with you, I will," I conceded. "That's all I have to offer right now."

Freddy offered a curt nod. "Fine. I'll take whatever I can get. There's only one person that comes to mind."

I held my breath as I waited for what he was about to say.

I prayed it might be the break we were looking for.

CHAPTER TWENTY

"BRUCE PATTERSON," FREDDY ANNOUNCED AS IF HE'D JUST given the winning answer on *Jeopardy* and knew he was going to take home an amazing monetary prize.

"Who is Bruce Patterson?" I supposed I'd expected to hear the name of someone I actually recognized. I had no idea who this Bruce guy was.

"You should check out his blog." Freddy's voice hitched as if the conversation excited him. "It's quite fascinating."

"Tell us a little more about this Bruce guy." Riley crossed his arms but his voice remained calm and non-accusatory.

Freddy let out a long breath. "Bruce is in his forties. Originally from California. But he's been obsessed with Milton Jones for years. He contacted me wanting some information."

"Information on what?" I asked, my hopes rising.

"Pretty much on anything I knew about Milton. Bruce was more than a little curious about every detail of the life of the Scum River Killer."

The Scum River Killer was what the media had taken to calling Milton Jones because of his proclivity to killing women and dumping them near that river in California.

"Did he strike you as the type who would want to pick up where Milton left off?" Riley asked.

Freddy's face went a little paler. "Whoa. What? That's sick."

"Tell me about it," I muttered. "But we're serious. Did he?"

He shook his head. "It's hard to say. I didn't delve into his psyche."

Riley placed his hand on my arm, as if he sensed my rising emotions. "Does this guy still live in California?"

"Last I heard, he did."

"And when is the last time you talked to him?" I asked.

Freddy shrugged and tugged the edge of his cap. "I don't know. Probably about a month ago. But he's been in contact with me more than once."

"What did you and Bruce talk about last time he contacted you?" I continued to push.

"Oh, that's easy. We talked about Milton's Last Stand."

Riley bristled again. "His last stand?"

"That's what some people call the very last crime Milton committed."

"Was there anything specifically he was asking about?" I stared at Freddy as I waited for his answer.

The man didn't even flinch as he looked me dead in the eye. "As a matter of fact, yes, there was. He was actually asking a lot of questions about you, Gabby."

A cold mass formed inside me as we drove away. That was the only way to describe the sensation lodged in my chest. I felt like a cannonball stored in dry ice had been placed beneath my skin, making it impossible for me to ever get warm again.

Riley waited until we were in our car before he turned to me. "Are you doing okay? Because you look like you might pass out."

"I'm not going to pass out." My hands fisted at my side. "What I'm going to do is I'm going to find this guy."

"Bruce?"

I shrugged. "It's a good starting place at least."

"I agree. We should definitely check out his blog."

I paused and let out a sigh, trying not to feel over-whelmed by the scope of what was happening. "I can't stop thinking about Sharon. About where she is. What she's going through. I want to find her."

"I know your impulse is to get out there on the streets and to search for her. But that's not going to do much good right now. Right now, let's do our homework. Let's look into this Bruce guy. Let's follow up with Parker and Adams. Then figure out what we're going to do."

I nodded, knowing that his words made sense. "I need to check on Sierra too. I can't stop thinking about little Reef without his mom if Sierra is arrested."

"There's definitely a lot going on." He reached over and squeezed my hand. "We're going to get through this."

I wanted to jump in and agree with him. But every time I closed my eyes, I remembered the day I'd heard the news that Riley had been shot and was in the hospital.

I couldn't stop thinking about it. Imagining it happening again.

And as soon as those thoughts crossed my mind, panic followed. Panic that I'd finally found the love of my life and now I faced the possibility of losing him again.

I knew that Riley and I weren't promised forever together. I knew that we weren't infallible. But I wanted more time with him. I couldn't bear the idea of a madman taking his life.

I fisted my hands again.

I was going to do everything within my power to stop this.

Everything, I vowed.

CHAPTER TWENTY-ONE

When I'd gotten back home, I checked on Sierra. She seemed to be doing okay, although she had that preoccupied look in her eyes. Who could blame her?

I sensed she might need some time alone with just Chad and Reef, so I slipped back over to my house. When I walked inside, Riley was sitting with his laptop at the kitchen table. I pulled up a chair beside him and stared at the screen.

Riley had managed to find Bruce Patterson's blog.

"Anything of note?" I asked, studying the screen.

"No, he says a lot, but he doesn't really say anything, if that makes sense. He mostly posts articles about Milton and what he did, almost like this is his personal idea board instead of something meant for the public."

"Creepy."

"Or crazy."

"Crazy as in obsessed, or crazy as in he wants to pick up where he left off and he blames me for the man's death?"

"I don't know. I'm afraid it's a little of both."

I heard the strain in Riley's voice. This was worrying him—as it would anyone in their right mind.

"Anything else I need to know about what you've seen?" I looked at the computer screen and saw Bruce's photo. I noted the man's long, stringy dark-blond hair. His premature wrinkles. But mostly, I saw his eyes.

I stared into those black eyes. I had seen eyes like that before. They were so cold. They belonged to someone who could hurt others without thinking twice.

I repressed a shudder.

I would never be able to get that image out of my mind.

Even though it was past ten o'clock and pitch-black outside, I couldn't sit in my house and pretend every-thing was normal while Sharon was possibly suffering at the hands of a madman.

I'd already called Adams and Parker, and they had no updates for me. I had peppered them with questions, some of which they answered and some of which they hadn't.

After pacing my bedroom, trying to think everything through, I finally turned to Riley. "I want to visit Sharon's house again."

He looked at me and pulled off his reading glasses. He'd been sitting in bed with his laptop, trying to research this Bruce guy.

"You know it's a crime scene, right?" he reminded me. "There's no way that the police are going to let you inside."

"I know. I want to see the neighborhood again, though. I want to maybe talk to her neighbors or look for security cameras or—"

"I'm sure the police have already done most of those things." Riley didn't sound edgy. Instead, his voice was quiet with a tender compassion.

"I know. But I'm not the police. Maybe that means I'll be able to find something they can't. I've always been able to use that to my advantage. Maybe it will work now."

"Okay then." He rose and took my hand. "Let's go."

"You're going to go with me?" He hadn't always been such a willing accomplice in these things.

"Of course. I'm not going to let my girl go out there and fight this battle alone."

Warmth spread through my chest. I stood on my tiptoes and planted a kiss on his cheek. I loved this man. I thanked God every day that He'd brought us together.

Riley loved me, even with all my issues and insecurities. I felt blessed far beyond what I deserved every time I looked at him.

I grabbed my jacket, ready to try to solve this crime with my partner in crime.

CHAPTER TWENTY-TWO

Riley didn't say much as we stood on the cracked sidewalk in front of Sharon's house. I stared at it now. I kept imagining Sharon inside. I kept trying to picture what may have happened to her last night or whenever she was taken.

I assumed it was last night, but it could've just as easily been this morning, I supposed. I hadn't seen any evidence to prove it either way.

I was thankful for the quiet because I needed time with my thoughts. I needed the pictures to play out in my head without interruption. I needed to use my skills of observation to make sure there was nothing we'd missed.

Sharon lived on an ordinary street in a blue-collar neighborhood. Little cottage-like houses built in the

1950s lined each road. Some were cute and well-maintained. Many were not.

Based on my earlier observations, all kinds of people lived in this neighborhood. Each home told a different story. Some were places with eight cars out front of a two-bedroom home, trash in the flower beds, and open windows with herbal smells drifting out. Others had clothes hanging on the line in the backyard and cheerful flags.

If somebody had come to Sharon's house, where had he parked? Had he pulled to the curb and then walked up to her front door?

A lot of people hung around outside, even at this hour. If someone had simply pulled in front of her home, it would have been a brazen move. Somebody on this block could easily have seen them.

I suppose that somebody could have pulled into her driveway too. Sharon's car was still there, but there was room behind it for one more vehicle. It would be a little easier to conceal what you were doing if you were parked there, especially if you had backed in.

But carrying out a body through the front door would still be risky.

"If I'd been the bad guy, I would have used the back door," I muttered.

"What was that?" Riley asked.

I snapped my attention back to him. "I am just trying to picture what happened here. I don't think this guy used the front door. There's no way he could get Sharon out the front door without somebody seeing something."

"What if Sharon was lucid? What if she just walked out and this guy had a gun to her, and he forced her to pretend everything was okay?"

"I guess that is a possibility also. Not sure if it's this guy's MO either."

"What did Milton Jones do when he captured you at the hospital?"

I shuddered as I told him about being Tasered. Stuffed into an oversized laundry cart by Milton, who'd disguised himself as a maintenance worker. Led outside while no one was the wiser.

As I recounted the story, that same cold ball of fear began to freeze inside me, spreading until it reached my veins.

I knew the fear Sharon was probably feeling right now.

That made finding her even more urgent.

Since there wasn't a police line around the house, Riley and I ventured into the backyard.

There was no garage, only a small shed in the corner that had seen better days. Lots of trees and brush grew up around it, making me wonder if Sharon ever even went inside the structure. I probably wouldn't.

She didn't have a deck behind her house, only three cement steps that led to a crooked door.

She'd painted that door bright pink, adding a little bit of her personality to it.

Another house stood directly behind hers with only a chain link fence separating the yards.

I stared at that house.

The windows were all dark. Was that because the inhabitants were sleeping? Or was it unoccupied?

I tried to picture the killer using that house. Climbing over the fence. Going to the back door. Picking the lock and sneaking inside.

Fear started to well in me, but I pushed it down.

"What are you thinking now?" Riley jammed his hands into his pockets.

"I'm thinking, if I'd been the one behind this crime, I would have carried Sharon across the yard and over the fence to a car that waited there. That way, I would have some privacy. It was probably the safest bet for getting away without being seen."

"Interesting."

If there was one thing that Milton Jones had been, it was careful. That trait had helped him get away with his crimes for so long. He didn't leave clues behind. Or the ones he left, I should say, were the ones that he *wanted* to leave so he could toy with investigators.

Just like he'd been toying with me when he left those clues inside that box.

No, *Milton* hadn't been toying with me, I corrected. But somebody else who greatly admired Milton Jones was.

I remembered Bruce Patterson's cold, heartless eyes.

Yes, somebody like Bruce could be responsible for this.

Just as the thought entered my head, I heard a stick break behind me.

Someone was here.

I reached for the gun in my purse as I twirled around.

CHAPTER TWENTY-THREE

"WHAT DO YOU TWO THINK YOU'RE DOING BACK HERE?"

My gaze locked onto the man who approached us, baseball bat in hand. The man had a bushy gray-and-white beard that looked as unkempt as his dirty clothing. Even in the dark, I could somehow sense the stains on his oversized sweatshirt.

Riley pushed me behind him and used his best negotiating voice as he said, "We don't mean any harm. We are friends of Sharon's."

The man stared at us, not bothering to hide the suspicion in his gaze. The good news was that he was not Bruce Patterson. The bad news was that he had a baseball bat and looked ready to use it.

My hand still remained on my gun. I prayed that I didn't have to use it.

"How do I know you're not here because you're the ones who hurt her?" The man's voice sounded gruff and rumbling.

"We're not," Riley said. "I'm an attorney, and Gabby is an investigator. We're trying to figure out what happened to Sharon. She's our friend."

"I can't sleep thinking about what she might be going through," I added.

Our words seemed to soften the man, and he lowered his bat. "Sharon's a good woman. I haven't been able to stop thinking about everything either."

"We've introduced ourselves," Riley said. "Do you mind sharing who you are?"

"I'm her neighbor." He leaned on the bat, using it like a cane. "Name is Einstein."

"Einstein?" I repeated.

"That's what my friends call me. My real name is Steve."

I liked Einstein better. It had personality. The man's crazy hair added a bit to the mad genius vibe.

"It seems like you like to keep an eye on Sharon," I started. "Did you happen to see anything or hear anything last night?"

"I wasn't home. I wish I had been. Maybe I could've stopped this." His voice broke, and he looked away.

I could tell this guy really did care about Sharon. I wondered if Einstein was married and this was just a friendly consideration, or if there was more to their story. Clarice said her aunt stayed home and didn't date. What if Sharon stayed home so she *could* date?

"How about this morning?" Riley asked. "Did you see or hear anything then?"

"I thought she was taken last night?" Einstein said.

"We haven't confirmed that yet." I still felt a measure of caution as I spoke with the man. Being too trusting had never proven to be a good thing. "We just know that Sharon disappeared sometime between dinner last night and this morning. It's an assumption that she was taken at night because it would be easier. That's not a guarantee."

"I see." He frowned and looked back at her house.

"What about this house behind us?" I pointed to the structure. "Does anybody live here?"

"There were renters in there for a long time," Einstein said. "They moved out about three months ago, and no one has lived there since."

It was abandoned. Good to know. "That's helpful. Thank you."

"I hope you two find this guy, and he gets the justice that he deserves. And if this guy did anything to hurt Sharon . . ." Einstein's nostrils flared, and he shook his head ever-so-slightly. "If he hurt my Sharon, I'm going to make him live to regret the day he stepped foot on this property."

I was glad to know that Sharon had people close by who watched out for her.

If we did find this guy—or *when* we found this guy, I should say—I was going to sic Einstein on him.

After Einstein left, Riley and I turned to each other. The nice part about being married was that sometimes all we had to do was look at each other and not say a thing, yet we still knew exactly what the other person was thinking.

Most of the time that worked. Sometimes we got it totally wrong. Like when I hinted that I wanted rocky road ice cream, and Riley somehow interpreted that as buffalo wings. But that was a story for another day.

"I think this guy used the backyard." I nodded at the house behind Sharon's.

"Do you think he carried Sharon over the fence?"

I stared at the chain-link structure. "I don't think this guy cares about anybody. I think he grabbed Sharon, maybe even Tased her, and then dropped her on the other side."

Riley flinched. "That sounds harsh."

"There's nothing kind about kidnapping or murder," I reminded him.

"I can't argue with that one."

I pulled up the flashlight on my phone and walked

over toward the fence. I was sure that the police had already checked this out.

In which case, there would be no harm in checking behind them.

Carefully, I inspected the metal links. I remember climbing fences like this when I was a child. Specifically, one time when I was probably eight and I'd been running away from a neighbor's dog when I climbed a fence like this. My shirt had gotten stuck on one of the pieces of metal, and I'd feared I wasn't going to be able to get away in time.

I finally managed to, but I ripped my shirt in the process. My dad hadn't been happy with me. Money had been tight, and I was down a shirt. I'd only owned seven, one for each day of the week.

I pushed those memories aside and inspected the center of the fence, the most obvious place that somebody would escape.

I paused and looked around. But maybe this was *too* obvious.

Because standing right here in the backyard, the streetlight from the road crept to this area and illuminated it.

If I was a killer, I wouldn't have used this spot.

I glanced up and down the length of the fence.

No, if I was the killer, I would've gone closer to the shed. The section was more hidden and darker.

Riley followed behind me as I walked that way. I

continued to shine my light on the fence, desperately hoping that I might find a clue of some sort.

"This is like looking for a needle in a haystack," Riley said.

"But you know what the good thing is about a needle in a haystack?"

"What's that?"

"There actually *is* a needle." I glanced back at him, determined to drive home my point. "If there's a needle here, I'm going to find it."

Riley grinned. "I've always loved that about you."

He didn't have much hope that I was going to find anything, and I really couldn't blame him. But I wouldn't be able to sleep tonight unless I did everything within my power to find Sharon.

As I got closer to the shed, the brush around it became thicker. Litter had become trapped in some of the branches and sprouts. Some cups. Strings. Wet tissues that looked like they had been there for weeks.

There are probably snakes in there too, but they should be sleeping at night, right? Did snakes sleep at night?

I was going to believe they did.

As I leaned closer, something caught the light off my flashlight.

It was a pink piece of thread.

Pink like the pink Sharon loved to wear.

Not only that, but it looked new. Fresh.

"Riley, look . . ."

Riley leaned closer. "Do you think that's Sharon's?"

"I think it's a good possibility," I told him. "But I'll let Adams figure that out."

CHAPTER TWENTY-FOUR

"So you think this is the way the killer got her away from the house without anyone seeing? Through the backyard and over this chain link fence?" Adams stared at me, waiting for my opinion.

I was honored.

Lights had been staged in the area, and the crime-scene crew had come back to further investigate.

The instructor part of me, the side who'd worked for Grayson Technologies training these people, wanted to have a heart-to-heart talk with each of these guys. I wanted to ask them how they could possibly missed this.

This was why I felt that I had to be nosy and do things on my own. I'd seen the police department fail too many times.

I wasn't patting myself on the back. I was by no

means perfect. But I *was* determined. I didn't think anyone could argue with that.

"What's your theory?" I asked Adams, deciding to try a different tactic.

"That this guy backed his car up to the victim's house under the cover of nightfall."

"This guy is smart. He would know there are too many neighbors watching. He had to go in the back way. If you look past this fence, in the neighbor's yard, I'm quite sure you're going to see some tire prints. And the house on that property has been unoccupied for three months."

Adams' eyebrows shot up. "You've been doing your research. For the record, we did go to that house earlier and knock on the door. Nobody answered."

"That doesn't mean there aren't clues on the property. Aren't you going to follow up? Check out the yard just in case?"

"Look, Gabby." Adams rubbed a hand over his face. "We're shorthanded. We're doing the best that we can."

"I'm not talking about a string of burglaries or someone who's spraying graffiti. I'm talking about a woman who is missing and who could be at the mercy of a ruthless killer. In cases like this, it doesn't hurt to check and double-check." I probably shouldn't sound so harsh, but how could I not? There was no good reason they'd missed this.

Adams gave me a look, and I knew I had stepped out of line.

I clamped my mouth shut, trying to remain respectful.

"Would you like to go with me to investigate this other house?" Adams said after a moment.

I couldn't believe he offered.

"I thought you'd never ask." I offered a winsome smile, hoping to show my gratitude.

He started toward the other place, and I followed behind him. Meanwhile, Riley stood where he was, watching the crime-scene techs.

Good. Maybe he'd make sure they didn't miss anything else.

Adams and I climbed over the fence. I did so a little more gracefully than Adams, but we both managed to make it.

Our flashlights scattered illumination in front of us as we studied the ground.

It had rained earlier today, so the ground was damp. The moisture may have washed away any clues that had been left.

We searched the perimeter of the house. But when we came to the driveway, that's when something really caught my eye.

Tire tracks. Just like I'd thought.

They veered off the driveway and into the yard. It would have been the perfect area for the killer to back into. He could have made a clean getaway, and none of the neighbors would have been the wiser for it.

When Adams' gaze met mine, I knew he was thinking the same thing.

Maybe this meant we were one step closer to finding some answers.

"If it isn't Gabby St. Claire Thomas."

I waved my hand in the air in a mini salute before stepping into Garrett Mercer's office the next morning. As I did, the scent of coffee surrounded me, along with the soothing sounds of a midafternoon shower in the rainforest. The ambient sound played on an overhead somewhere.

I gripped my free coffee that I'd picked up on my way in.

That was a perk for visiting the Global Coffee Initiative, I supposed.

Last night, as I had been trying to go to sleep, I realized that there was one name I'd left off my earlier list.

Garrett's.

I'd met him when Milton Jones had forced himself into my life.

Riley had been representing Garrett in a case, and some crazy connections had popped up between Garrett and the whole Milton Jones fiasco.

Today, Garrett and I were good friends. He funded my cold-case squad, and I thought the world of him.

There was nothing not to love about the man with his British accent and charming disposition. That wasn't to mention the fact that he was wildly successful in the coffee business and he had a heart for philanthropy.

"To what do I owe this honor? Do you have a new case to present to me?" He leaned back in his chair as he waited for my answer.

I sat across from him and shook my head. "I wish my visit was about a cold case. I suppose, in some ways, it might be considered that."

He straightened, making it clear that I had his undivided attention now. "What's going on, Gabby?"

I explained the events of the last several days. As I did, Garret's face became more and more stoic.

"I'm so sorry, Gabby. I know this must be hard for you. I can only imagine . . ."

I nodded, probably a little too quickly. "It all feels surreal."

"You do know this guy's going to come after you, don't you?"

My blood went cold again. "Yes, but I'm more afraid of him going after Riley."

Realization dawned in his eyes. "I can't believe this is happening."

"Believe me, I can't either."

"So what can I do for you?"

I drew in a deep breath before starting. "I'm revisiting everybody who had any part in Milton Jones's case. I firmly believe that whoever is behind this is connected with the man."

Garrett raised an eyebrow. "So, you think that I might be behind this?"

I quickly shook my head. "No, I think I know you well enough to know you wouldn't do something like this."

But even as I said the words, I had to wonder—did you ever really know someone that well? I didn't want to think that anybody I knew could be responsible. Not Adams. Not Parker. Nobody I had any type of relationship with.

But when those thoughts crossed my mind, was I putting on my blinders? Was I ruling out people who shouldn't be ruled out?

As I stared at Garrett with his dark hair and sparkly eyes, I had to wonder that also.

Then guilt flooded me. What kind of friend was I to doubt the people around me?

Needless to say, sometimes the answers weren't as black-and-white as we might like for them to be.

I cleared my throat. "Is there anyone else you can remember from that investigation that might help us?"

Garrett remained silent for a moment before shaking his head. "I wish I had something, Gabby. I really do. But I've got nothing."

Even though I'd expected that answer, disappointment still pressed on me. "If you think of anything, can you let me know?"

"Of course. You know that whatever you need me to do to help, I'll do it."

I had no doubt that Garrett meant those words. But I wished I was leaving his office with a clue.

CHAPTER TWENTY-FIVE

MY THOUGHTS WERE STILL HEAVY AS I WANDERED OUT TO my car, which was parked behind Garrett's downtown office building.

Riley had gone into work today. He had a court case he couldn't miss. I knew if I really needed him, he would have stayed home. But I didn't want him to do that.

Instead, I'd promised to be careful. Riley had given me a look that clearly stated he knew me well enough to know that careful was not something I was good at, especially when my friends' lives were on the line.

But I was going to do my best. It was bright daylight, and I tried to remain aware of everything around me.

At least Sierra hadn't been arrested yet.

She was working from home today, and Chad was

working with her. We hadn't been called to any crime scenes, so that was another positive.

Part of me had hoped that Adams or Parker would have called me with an update if there had been any, but I knew I was hoping for too much. I wasn't officially a part of this investigation, and it didn't matter how many training sessions I did for Grayson Tech. Unless I was on the police force or a member of the FBI, I was going to be an outsider. That was pretty much my middle name. Gabby Let-Me-In-from-the-Cold Thomas.

I really needed to figure out a plan for my future. I couldn't keep cleaning crime scenes. As much as part of me liked it, I knew I had bigger things planned for me.

But what?

Should I keep waiting for more opportunities with Grayson Tech?

That idea didn't excite me.

Should I apply to work as a CSI with a local department?

Maybe. But, in my gut, I didn't think that's where I was going to end up.

I thought about that body I'd found in the attic. Thought about the signs of decomposition I'd seen. Stuff like that fascinated me.

A coroner? I wasn't sure I could see myself doing that either.

But I needed to figure something else out.

Because solving crime was in my blood. It was what I'd been created to do.

It was time for a pivot in my life.

As I reached my car, I hit the key fob and heard the beep as my car unlocked. But I paused beside the door, my instincts telling me that something was amiss around me.

With a stiff neck, I turned around, looking for the source of my stress.

I scanned all the cars. The streets. The other office buildings.

Nothing stood out. Nothing obvious, at least.

Sometimes you had to look for the obvious—because it was the best place to hide answers. But other times, you had to look at the details.

This was one of those times I needed to look at the details.

I opened my car door as insurance that I could jump inside quickly if needed.

Then I scanned everything around me again.

My second scan didn't offer additional information.

As I examined the area a third time, I noticed someone sitting in a car two rows over.

His windows were dark, tinted. But not so tinted that I couldn't see anything.

I could clearly see a man inside.

That man was unmistakably looking at me.

I squinted, desperate to make out more details.

Before I could, the car jerked out from its space.

As it did, the driver rolled down his window.

Bruce Patterson stared back at me.

.

CHAPTER TWENTY-SIX

I ONLY LET SHOCK CONSUME ME FOR A FEW SECONDS.

Then I jumped into action.

This was my chance to catch this guy. Not that I had any idea what I would do if I did manage to stop him. I'd probably end up dying, which would defeat the purpose of catching him.

Semantics.

Either way, I knew I couldn't let him drive away.

I jumped into my car and cranked the engine. Several seconds later, I tore through the parking lot.

I could still see the rundown burgundy-colored sedan. The driver had gone left out of the lot.

As I turned after him, I hit the Bluetooth on my phone and dialed Adams. He answered on the first ring, and I quickly gave him the update as to what was going on.

"Stand down, Gabby." A fatherly tone stained his voice. "I'll put an APB out on this man's car. You don't confront him."

"I just don't want to lose him." I craned my neck, still trying to see him.

"Get his plates and let us do the rest."

"I can't let him get away," I muttered.

"Gabby . . ."

"I'll be careful. I promise." Before Adams could argue with me anymore, I ended the call.

I threaded my way after the man, cutting down the streets of downtown Norfolk. Somehow, Bruce managed to get about two blocks ahead of me.

Two blocks of city streets were different than two blocks any other place.

But I kept my eyes on the car.

So far, so good. No traffic lights had separated us.

But I didn't know how long that would last.

I gripped my steering wheel as my heart pounded in my ears.

That man had been following me. Maybe Bruce *was* behind these crimes the whole time. It certainly beat my theory that Adams or Parker might be responsible.

As a car in front of Bruce slowed to turn, I gained some distance.

Excitement surged in me.

Maybe this was my chance. Maybe I'd catch up with him. Just to get his license plate number, of course. Then again, what were the chances that this guy's license plate numbers were actually his? We already knew his name, so I didn't know how much running his plates would tell us. At least it would be *something*.

I gained more ground. For once, things were working out in my favor.

Two cars were between us. But if I could just get around them, I could catch up with this guy.

Just then, one of the cars took a right-hand turn onto a side street.

Yes!

I could feel it in my bones.

I might actually get some answers.

Just as Bruce began to slow at a yellow light, I hit my brakes, watching carefully to see what he would do.

As the light turned red, he stopped.

This was it. There was only one car in between us. Should I jump out of the driver's seat and confront him?

That seemed like a bad idea.

Instead, I pulled out my phone and tried to take a picture of the license plate. But the other car was too close. I couldn't see it.

I nibbled on my lip, trying to figure out what to do.

As I did, the light turned green.

That had been fast. Too fast.

I prepared myself to keep following him.

But before I could, a crossing guard appeared in front of me, hand raised with a stop sign out front.

Crossing guard?

I glanced beside me and saw a school in the distance. I'd been so focused on following Bruce that I hadn't even taken note of my surroundings.

As Bruce pulled forward, my foot remained on the brake. A line of elementary school students crossed in front of me as I watched my one lead disappear down the road.

As I drove, my thoughts remained on Sharon. I wished I knew how to find her. I didn't know where to go after I lost Bruce, and I didn't want to drive around aimlessly.

So I did the next best thing.

I headed home.

The last thing I wanted to do was to sit around twiddling my thumbs. There had to be something I could do. There *had* to be something I was missing.

Why had Bruce made himself known to me? He was playing a game, I realized. But why let me see his cards? It didn't make sense.

I called Adams, and he didn't have any updates for me. He only assured me his officers were out looking for Bruce.

As soon as I walked into my house, I realized what I

needed to do. But I also knew that I couldn't do it on my own.

Bile rose in me when I thought about the place where I needed to go.

I needed to visit the cabin where Milton Jones had held me captive.

It was a dilapidated shack in the Dismal Swamp area of the region. I felt like going there would give me a good case of PTSD.

But what if that was where Sharon was being held? I knew it was probably a long shot. But something told me it was worth checking out.

I supposed I could simply call law enforcement and send them out there. But they wouldn't see what I saw. I'd been there. I'd lived out some of my worst hours there.

As memories rushed at me, I walked into my house and greeted Watson. My phone rang at the same time. It was Riley, and he was right on time. Maybe he would put a halt to the bad ideas I toyed with. But did I really want him to?

"I just got out of court, and I thought I might head home a little early."

"That would be great. Because there's something I need to do, and I need you to be with me." I refilled Watson's water bowl and waited for Riley's response.

"I thought you might need a sidekick today."

A sidekick? I smiled at the sound of that. Riley was anything but a sidekick. He was a partner.

"That sounds great," I told him. "I'll explain everything once you get here."

As I waited for him, I went into the bedroom to change my shoes. No way would I wear flip-flops in a swampy area.

As I sat down on the edge of the bed, one of my earrings caught on a curl and slipped from my lobe. As I reached under the bed to retrieve it, my fingers brushed a paper.

Out of curiosity, I sank to my knees to take a better look. As far as I knew, nothing was stored under our bed. Riley was too much of a neat freak to let that happen.

An old news article lay on the floor.

When I read the headline, my breath caught.

The article was on Milton Jones and his final hours.

Of course, I was mentioned in it. I'd forever go down in history as the woman who'd almost been his last victim.

As I glanced up, my breath caught.

A folder was wedged between the mattress and box spring.

Carefully, I pulled it out.

Inside, there were uncountable articles about Milton Jones.

Why had Riley been studying these? How long had

they been here? Even more so, why did he feel the need to hide them from me?

I remembered that sinking feeling I'd had that maybe the person behind this was someone that I knew.

I shook my head.

No, that thought was crazy. Riley would never, ever do something like this. I trusted him with my life. I wasn't even sure where the lightning bolt-like thought had come from.

I shook my head again, as if trying to dislodge the idea and pretend that it had never happened.

How could I even think something like that about my spouse? I loved Riley, and he loved me. Sure, that brain injury he'd sustained had changed him. But not like this. Not into someone totally different.

But I was still bothered . . . bothered by the reality that the thought had even popped into my head.

CHAPTER TWENTY-SEVEN

AN HOUR LATER, WE WERE IN CHAD'S OLD WORK VAN, surrounded by the scent of cleaning supplies and old fast food.

Chad was in the driver's seat with Sierra beside him. Meanwhile, Riley and I sat in the second row with Sir Watson. Reef was with a sitter for a couple of hours.

For a moment, I felt like we were trying to channel the cast of *Scooby-Doo*. Despite that, I was glad my friends were here with me.

When I'd told Riley what I wanted to do, Chad and Sierra had insisted that they wanted to come. They wanted answers about this investigation just as much as anyone. I couldn't blame them for that, especially when Sierra's future might be on the line, and then, by default, Chad's and Reef's as well.

I didn't mention the articles I'd found to Riley. Not yet. I would wait.

But I was still disturbed that I'd even questioned him in my mind. Not just disturbed, but I was guilt-ridden. He deserved a wife who fully supported him.

Then again, I *did* fully support him. One fleeting thought didn't change that.

My thoughts continued their battle until I felt a headache coming on.

"Have you heard anything else about this bomb that went off?" I finally asked Sierra.

"The police questioned me and then questioned my coworkers," Sierra said. "They looked at my bank accounts. I know they didn't find anything. Sure, it was suspicious that I was at Cityside when I was, but that doesn't mean I set the bomb."

"The thing I've been wondering is how did this person who's truly responsible know that you were going to be at Cityside that day?" I asked.

"It's interesting that you ask that because I actually got an email that exposed some of the dastardly practices taking place at Cityside Seafood." Sierra frowned as she pushed her glasses up.

My blood went a little colder. "When did you get that?"

"About four days ago."

"That was risky," I mused aloud. "The email could have gotten lost. How did this person know that you were going to be there on a Saturday? And if you hadn't gone on a Saturday, would they have done the same thing when people were there?"

Sierra frowned again. "I don't know. But the email I got did say something about Saturday being a good day to check out their operations. Something about the supervisors being more available."

"So the sender planted the thought that you should go on a Saturday." I shook my head, again realizing just how smart the person behind this was. "I suppose you already told the authorities about it."

"I did. There's no need to hold back anything. Not when I already look guilty."

"I wonder if they have any other suspects in their sights . . ." I didn't bother to keep any of my thoughts inside my head.

"I have no idea. But I feel like the clock is ticking and it's just a matter of time before they somehow think that I am the person responsible for this." Sierra's voice broke, giving us a glimpse of what was going on inside her.

I couldn't even imagine how terrified she must feel.

I reached forward and squeezed her shoulder. "I'm sorry."

"I'm sorry too. I still can't get over how things went from peaceful and normal to totally chaotic and a mess." She stared out the window, her hand going over her belly.

Her belly where a precious baby was growing inside.

"I think we're all in that boat," Riley said. "Whoever is behind these crimes has been planning them for a while. There's no way he wasn't. All the details have been planned and meticulous. Whoever did this, he knows all about Gabby. Some of the mysteries she's solved have been written up in the newspapers, but others haven't. Plus, this guy knows how much she likes music."

"Are you suggesting that this guy has an inside track?" Surprise sliced through Chad's voice.

"Not necessarily," Riley said. "But there's some connection there. We just need to figure out what."

That was what Riley had been doing with his articles, hadn't it? He'd been trying to find that connection.

Relief flooded through me.

I should have assumed that from the start. Once paranoia had set in, those thoughts wanted to take over. To grow and grow until you didn't realize how big your suspicions had become.

I could have laughed at myself, but I didn't want to draw attention to my assumption.

As we traveled, we left the city behind, and the roads around us turned into pure country. The landscape was full of unending trees with the occasional farmhouse in between.

As I glanced at the woods, I noticed the pools of dark water that had settled at the roots of various trees.

I shuddered. Something about the swamp had always creeped me out.

This was no different.

I lifted a prayer and tried to brace myself for whatever was about to come.

I caught myself nearly hyperventilating as I stared at the cabin where Milton had brought me.

The structure was tiny—probably only eight feet square. Inside, the floors were concrete. There were no windows.

Since I'd last been here, ivy had grown up the wood-sided walls. Weeds lined the edges. Part of the roof had blown off.

Memories began to slam into me until I felt like I had just been in a fistfight. With a hangover. While having the flu.

Riley slipped his arm around my waist. "Are you okay?"

I nodded. I had no choice but to nod. I had to be okay. If we wanted answers, there would be no feeling sorry for myself. I had to push through this.

"Just lots of bad memories," I finally said.

"I can only imagine. I'm sorry you have to go through this. Do you prefer that we go inside and you wait out here for us?"

I shook my head, but my neck felt stiff. I stood behind my earlier assertion. I was the best person for the job when it came to looking for anything out of place. I was the one who was familiar with this old shack.

"This is the first time I've seen this place." Sierra pushed her glasses up on her nose and frowned. "Seeing it makes what happened to you all too real."

"I'm glad you've never seen it before, and I'm sorry that you have to see it now." My words sounded somber. As much as I wanted to force myself to sound cheerful, I couldn't.

Chad let out a deep breath before turning to us. "Should we go inside?"

"I guess we should." I held onto Sir Watson's leash, glad the dog was with me. Riley made me feel the safest, but Sir Watson was a close second.

Dread pooled in my stomach as I stepped inside the dark, dark place—not dark only because of the absence of light. But dark because of what had happened here.

I reached for the light switch, knowing the electricity had probably been turned off.

The black space stared back at me.

Everything looked even worse than I remembered from when I'd been held captive here.

Riley pulled up the flashlight on his phone and scanned the room.

Same cement floor. Dirty walls.

Were those scratches on the door?

Nausea rose in me as more memories hit. Memories of being held here. Of smelling death.

Not other people's death.

My own.

"Is there anything here that strikes you?" Riley asked quietly.

I waited for something to hit me. For some kind of clue to show me the way. To give a clear indication of what was going on.

But so far, there had been nothing.

"No, everything basically looks the same."

I stepped into the room where Juliette Barnes and I had been kept. I glanced around the small space one more time. The room was plain, with no windows or other means of escape. I remembered being awakened when my head had been submerged in a bucket of freezing cold water. I remembered feeling trapped. How much my body ached after Jones tried to strangle me.

Right now, nothing was here except some leaves that had fallen through the opening in the ceiling.

What a disappointment.

"You ready?" Riley placed a hand on my back as if trying to tread carefully.

I nodded. "I'd like to walk around the outside also."

We stepped outside, and I paced with Sir Watson across the ground. It was mostly dry here with an over-abundance of weeds. Dead leaves on the ground added a crispiness to our steps.

I paused as I started toward the backside of the cabin.

We weren't far from the very area where Milton Jones died, I realized. It was just to my left, probably fifty feet deeper into the woods.

I shivered at the memories but didn't let them consume me.

I continued pacing instead. As I crossed the back of the building, I sucked in a breath.

There, painted in red spray paint on the back was a message. For me.

It read:

The Closer I Get to You.

Beside it was a smiley face—a symbol that clearly told me the killer was enjoying every moment of this game.

CHAPTER TWENTY-EIGHT

I CALLED CLARICE ON THE WAY HOME TO MAKE SURE SHE was doing okay.

Even though her voice sounded strained, she said she was doing as well as could be expected. She was spending time with some friends today, and they were taking care of her.

Just as I wrapped up that conversation, someone called in.

Parker.

I clicked over to him.

"I have good news," he announced.

"I could use some good news." I stared out the window, trying to get the cryptic message out of my head. I'd already called Adams and told him about the message. He was supposed to be getting in touch with Parker.

Was that what the special agent was calling about?

"I know you thought that we weren't going to be forthcoming with any details, but I thought I might just share this news," Parker started. "We located the boy who delivered the package to your house."

My heart skipped a beat. "You did?"

"He lives a couple of streets over. He told me some middle-aged guy paid him to take the package to your house at a certain time. The boy was instructed to leave it, knock on the door, and run."

My heart continued to pound in my chest. "Can he identify this guy?"

"We're talking to the boy now, and I'm trying to get a sketch."

"That's great news," I told him. "Thank you for letting me know."

"Are you at your house now?"

I glanced out the window again, trying to get my bearings. "We're almost there."

"I'm going to meet you there. I have a few more questions for you."

"That sounds good. I'll see you then."

I gave the rest of the gang the update. Several minutes later, we pulled up to the house and climbed out. I felt better knowing we were making *some* progress.

I hoped Parker would let me see the sketch. I could

only assume that this person who'd been IDed looked like Bruce Patterson. He made the most sense.

Chad and Sierra disappeared into the guest house, and Riley walked ahead so he could let Sir Watson loose in the backyard.

Before I even made it to the porch, Parker appeared farther down on the sidewalk. He must have decided to stretch his legs instead of driving.

A boy, who looked to be about ten, walked beside him, chatting his ear off. The boy had dark skin and wore a red hat and matching red tennis shoes.

Had this been the kid who'd delivered the package? He was literally a boy.

The killer had involved a little kid.

A chill went down my spine.

That boy probably had no idea what kind of evil he'd been face-to-face with.

Parker paused in front of me. "Gabby, this is Peter. Peter, Gabby. Peter is the one who left the package on your porch. I told him he didn't have to come with me to talk to you, but he wanted to anyway."

"I'm sorry." Peter looked up at me and frowned. "I didn't mean to start any trouble. That man said there was chocolate inside for you. How was I to know differently?"

"It's okay. Don't you worry about it." I smiled at him. The sincerity in the boy's tone did something to my heart. He was just as much a victim here as anyone.

Parker held up a picture. "This is a rough sketch the forensic artist put together of the man Peter talked to."

Rough was definitely a good description of the drawing. I couldn't make out anything about the man except that he was Caucasian and wore a baseball cap and sunglasses.

"We're going to do a more detailed sketch back at the office," Parker said. "Maybe we'll be able to ID this guy."

"That would be one good thing that could come out of this." I turned back to the boy with Parker. "So it was a middle-aged man?"

Peter nodded. "He wore a hat pulled down low over his face, so I couldn't see him very well. He also had on sunglasses and a sweatshirt."

"What kind of sweatshirt?" I asked, wondering if that might possibly be a clue.

"One with 'Georgetown' on the front."

"Georgetown?" I repeated, a nagging feeling beginning to form at the back of my mind.

"Yeah, that's right. Georgetown."

I swallowed hard, trying to make sense of my thoughts.

There was only one person I knew who wore Georgetown sweatshirts.

Because it was his alma mater.

As Riley stepped back outside, the boy raised his arm and pointed.

"It was him," Peter said. "He's the one who asked me to leave the package."

"Whoa." Riley raised his hands. "No offense, kid, but I've never seen you before."

"But it was you. You stopped me on the sidewalk and gave me twenty dollars to deliver the package."

Riley shook his head, his eyes widening with disbelief. "It wasn't me. You've got the wrong person."

"But you're wearing a Georgetown sweatshirt," Peter insisted.

"I don't remember the last time I wore this shirt." Riley turned to me. "Right, Gabby?"

"I can't remember the last time either." But part of me still felt ill as the boy's words replayed in my head, especially as I remembered my earlier doubts after I'd found those articles.

Parker's gaze darkened as he turned to my husband. "Is there anything you want to say, Riley?"

"Only that I absolutely did not do this." Riley sliced his hand through the air.

"And he's not middle-aged," I said. How could we overlook that fact?

"Yes, he is." Peter's tone suddenly filled with what could only be described as 'tude. "You guys are *old*. Do

you have grandkids yet? Does your house smell like
mothballs?"

"What? No." *Did* my house smell like mothballs? I'd
put some in one of my closets after we'd found, well . . .
moths inside. I needed to immediately remove them, I
realized.

Since when was being in your early thirties considered old?

As if that was my biggest worry right now.

I turned back to Peter. "You said the guy had on a
hat and sunglasses. How can you be so sure it's Riley if
you could hardly see his face?"

The boy shrugged. "I don't know. The same size and
height."

Parker glanced at Riley, who shook his head. His
hackles were obviously rising as more of the attention
was focused on him.

"Why would I send that to my wife?" Riley asked,
his normally placid voice turning demanding.

"That's a good question." Parker narrowed his eyes.
"Why would you? You would have known when
everyone would be here. You wouldn't have looked
guilty. Plus, whoever is behind this knows all about
Gabby."

Riley bristled. "I think you're out of line here, Parker.
You know I would never do anything to hurt Gabby."

Riley's words were said with such deep conviction

that it brought a shudder down my spine. He'd left no room for doubt as to how much he cared about me.

Another round of guilt washed over me. For the second time today, I'd questioned my husband's innocence.

I should be ashamed—and I was. But I reminded myself the important thing was that just because the thought entered my mind didn't mean I had to dwell on it. If thoughts were a location then I was just going to keep passing through instead of setting up residence.

Parker passed another glance at Riley and me before turning back to Peter. "You should go home now. I'll be in touch, okay?"

The boy nodded. "Sounds good. I'll be waiting."

As he scurried down the sidewalk, Parker turned toward us. His gaze had turned serious again. "Now that I have you two alone, there are a couple of things I want to talk to you about."

CHAPTER TWENTY-NINE

"We've been looking into this Bruce Patterson guy," Parker said.

Parker, Riley, and I sat around the dining room table. Everything felt stiff and marred with tension. I didn't expect anything otherwise.

"I heard you had a confrontation with him in the parking lot earlier today." Parker turned to me.

I remembered the look in Bruce's eyes as he'd stared at me from his window, and a shiver wiggled down my spine. "I did. You have an update?"

"It turns out he left his home about a week ago, and no one has seen or heard from him since."

"That's because he came here." I crossed my arms.

No one was going to convince me that Riley was guilty and that this man's presence here was a coincidence. I'd argue with anyone who tried until I made a presidential election debate look like child's play.

Parker didn't look amused as his eyelids tightened, and he tapped his foot. "We're trying to figure out where he's staying. But his cell phone was left at home, and he hasn't used any credit cards."

"Were you able to find out anything about his car?" Riley asked.

Parker shook his head. "From the sound of it, he drove his car here from California. The description matches. But if he thinks we're onto him, then he could have switched his vehicle by now. Either way, police in the area are on the lookout for him."

"That's good news, I guess." I wished I sounded more enthusiastic than I did.

"But there's also bad news." Parker grimaced. "This guy has a reputation for being violent. He beat up his neighbor over a disagreement about a tree. He has been in bar fights. He even had some citations for road rage. He's not somebody you want to tangle with."

"Believe me, I have no illusions of that." I shifted in my seat and leaned down to rub Watson's head. "What do I do in the meantime?"

"You sit tight. This guy is obviously watching you. We don't know how far he'll take it."

This guy. He didn't think Riley had anything to do with this either.

Someone had set up my husband.

Just like he'd set up Sierra.

I could only imagine what else this guy had up his sleeve.

"Do you think he has Sharon?" I held my breath as I waited for Parker's answer.

Parker's expression tightened. "We can't say for sure, of course, but it's a good possibility. That's why we're even more desperate to find out this guy's location."

Riley leaned forward, his elbows on the table and his gaze on Parker. "What do you make out of what that boy told you? You don't really think that I paid him to send that package, do you?"

Parker stared at Riley and didn't say anything for several seconds. Finally, he broke out of his trance-like state and said, "Honestly? No, I don't think you would do something like this. But maybe it was someone who looked like you."

"But Bruce Patterson does not look like me." Riley's words hung in the air.

He made a good point. The two looked nothing alike.

"If Patterson is involved with this, and that boy is telling the truth, then the only possibility is that Bruce is working with somebody." Parker let his words hang in the air.

His statement didn't make me feel any better. Two psychos out there? That was *not* comforting.

Parker sucked in a deep breath, suddenly looking exhausted. "In the meantime, I want to let you know that we're doing everything we can to find your friend. How many days did Milton Jones hold his victims before he killed them?"

"Six." My voice came out sharper than I'd intended.

That meant that our time was running out.

"This is all a mess." I leaned into Riley, putting my head on his shoulder as we sat on the couch together.

I wanted to get back out there. I wanted to storm the streets and keep trying to find this Bruce guy. Keep trying to track down Sharon.

But the truth was, I had no idea where to go or where to look.

I didn't like that answer, but it was the truth.

I was at a loss as to how to find my friend.

"This is definitely a mess," Riley said. "If somebody paid that kid to leave the package and he was wearing the same kind of sweatshirt that I have, then this person was trying to set me up."

That's what I thought also. "But why would someone do that?"

"My best guess? To mess with your head."

"Well, he's doing a good job."

Riley pulled back slightly. "You actually thought I sent that package?"

I scoffed at the idea. "Of course not."

There was no way I could tell him that, for three seconds flat, I might have considered the possibility. Three seconds wasn't enough to justify seriously considering anything.

"I do have a question for you, though." I decided to change the subject.

Riley stared down at me, his eyes warm and prodding. "What's that?"

Those warm and prodding eyes made it even harder for me to ask my question. But I knew I had no other choice.

"I dropped my earring today, and I happened to find a folder full of articles on Milton Jones stuck between our mattress and box spring," I said. "Why did you hide the articles there?"

I watched Riley's expression, trying to figure out exactly what he was thinking.

His jaw tightened, and his eyelids closed just slightly at my words. He hadn't wanted me to find those things. But why?

"I *have* been looking into him." Riley's voice almost contained a sigh-like quality. "You know that trial was one of the turning points in my life. Nothing was ever the same afterward."

"No, it wasn't."

"Now, it's almost like Milton wants to come back from the grave and make sure that nothing is the same still today. Someone is threatening you as well as people we care about. I want to find the guy who's responsible just as much as anyone else."

"But why hide the articles? That's what doesn't make sense to me." I couldn't end this conversation without knowing that.

"I wasn't exactly trying to hide them." Riley turned toward me, something in his gaze begging for my understanding. "I just know that it was a really hard time in your life also. I didn't want to stir up bad memories any more than necessary. I was hoping that by reading those articles something would ring a bell. Then I could present that information to you rather than subjecting you to all of those details again. A lot of those articles were about you. I'm sure you don't want to relive that."

His words made sense. Of *course*, that was the explanation. I wasn't sure why my mind had gone anywhere else but there.

I lowered my head onto Riley's shoulder again.

I didn't have anything else to say.

Right now, I just needed to contend with my thoughts.

CHAPTER THIRTY

I AWOKE THE NEXT MORNING TO FLASHING LIGHTS OUTSIDE my house. Instantly, my muscles tightened as I prepared myself for another round of bad news.

I nudged Riley beside me, and he opened his sleepy eyes. "What's going on?"

"That's what I would like to know," I rushed. "The police are outside."

We hopped out of bed and threw on some more presentable clothing before dashing outside.

Two police cars were parked in front of our home, along with an unmarked sedan.

I spotted Adams standing in the distance, a frown on his face. Once I saw him, I was certain something was majorly wrong.

I opened my mouth, about to ask him questions. Before I could, two officers led a handcuffed Sierra from the backyard. Chad trailed behind them, Reef in his arms. He didn't try to stop them.

Instead, he looked defeated with his slumped shoulders and worried gaze. Maybe he was trying to be strong for Reef so he could keep the boy calm.

I, on the other hand, did not have that much self-control.

I rushed toward my friend. "Sierra . . . what's going on?"

The officers didn't stop but continued to guide her toward the squad car in the distance.

"I didn't do it, Gabby." Sierra's voice pitched with fear.

"They think you bombed that building?" That was the only thing that made sense.

"They claim they have evidence."

The officers stopped at the car, and Adams motioned for them to put Sierra inside.

But I wasn't finished asking questions!

It didn't appear to matter. They secured her in the back of the car and closed the door. Tears glistened in my friend's eyes as she stared at me from the other side of the window.

Panic ripped through me. Sierra could *not* take the fall for this crime. I'd hoped since a couple of days had passed that meant the police had moved on and tried to find the real suspect here.

Obviously not.

I stormed back over to Adams. "Why are you arresting her? She didn't do this."

Adams sighed. "We discovered she has a paid storage unit about ten minutes from here—something she failed to mention to us. We went inside and discovered bomb-making materials that matched those that were used for the one that exploded at Cityside Seafood."

My head swam at his news. "There's got to be some mistake . . ."

Adams shook his head. "It's no mistake. We now have enough evidence to charge Sierra with a crime. Not only was she on the scene, but she has the materials to make the bomb and she has motive. I'm sorry, Gabby. I know this is not what you want to hear."

"But—"

Before I could say anything else, he strode back to his sedan.

Chad and Reef joined me at the curb as we watched them pull away.

I turned to Chad, remorse filling me. "I'm so sorry, Chad."

He held Reef closer, a far-off look in his eyes. He was obviously stunned—as anyone would be.

Then he said, "You should be. Sierra wouldn't be in jail right now if it wasn't for you, Gabby."

I opened my mouth to say something—I wasn't sure what—but, before I could, Chad stormed away.

I felt Riley behind me. He placed his hand on my shoulder.

But it didn't matter.

Nothing he could say or do would change things.

I felt like dirt. Like crime-scene sludge. Like the dirt that settled into the crime-scene sludge.

And all my efforts to make things right had been unsuccessful.

It appeared my friends would pay the price for my failures.

"Someone set up Sierra." I buried my face in my hands as I sat on the couch with Riley beside me several minutes later. "It's the only thing that makes sense."

That thought pounded through my skull on repeat until I couldn't think straight.

Riley had offered to go to the station and represent Sierra as her lawyer. Chad had refused and said we'd already done enough. Apparently, Chad was angry with Riley since Riley was married to me.

This couldn't be happening.

But it was.

I felt so powerless to do anything—and that wasn't okay with me. I'd overcome a lot in my life. Would this be the thing that defeated me?

I raised my chin.

No. I wouldn't let that happen.

"I agree that Sierra was set up," Riley murmured. "But who else knew about that storage facility?"

I could tell the thoughts were turning over in his head. His analytical side was trying to find a solution. His husband persona was trying to make me feel better. His kind heart was trying to ensure justice was served.

"We are the only ones who helped Chad and Sierra move their stuff in there," I said. "You and I and Tommy." Tommy was Chad's other employee, the one who currently had a broken leg.

Riley shook his head, looking like he was having trouble processing all this also. He leaned forward on the couch and ran a hand through his hair. "Somebody else must have discovered it and used it to their advantage."

"Or whoever is guilty is closer than I think." My words sent a subtle aftershock through the room. I knew I couldn't say something like that without those results. "Just like the clue said."

Riley studied my face. "What are you thinking, Gabby?"

I shook my head, not wanting any of the words to leave my lips. But I couldn't stay quiet anymore. It would do no good to protect someone out of loyalty.

I cleared my throat before asking, "What if it's Adams? Or Parker?"

Riley's eyes widened. "You mentioned them earlier.

But why would either of them do something like this? They don't have motive, means, or opportunity."

"I beg to differ. Both of them have opportunity. Both of them are privy to the details of the case. Both of them are also privy to information that the rest of us can't get. We don't know where they've been or what they've been doing. Maybe they *have* had the opportunity to do these things. They knew what kind of bomb was left in that building. They could have set up the supplies in that storage facility so Sierra would look guilty."

"You've really thought this through."

I shrugged. "Maybe."

"How about the why? *Why* would they do that?"

I thought about the question for a moment before sighing and shrugging. I grabbed a throw pillow from beside me and pulled it into my lap. "I'm going to sound arrogant if I say this, but . . ."

"Go ahead."

"But . . . maybe they resent me because I have solved cases they haven't." As soon as I said the words, I felt foolish. Would either of them really stoop that low?

Riley slowly bobbed his head up and down. "Maybe. But one of them would have had to build up *a lot* of resentment for that to be the case."

"People have had stranger motives."

Riley didn't argue with my statement—instead he expertly changed the subject. "What about this Bruce guy? Do you not think he's a part of this anymore?"

"Maybe he has an accomplice."

"Well, if his accomplice is either Adams or Parker, then something's wrong. Neither of those men look like me, not even to a ten-year-old boy who clearly needs glasses."

Riley had a point. I was just spinning in circles right now but going nowhere.

I had to make some progress here—especially since one friend was in jail and another missing, presumably taken by a serial killer.

Who was next?

I wished I hadn't asked myself that question.

Because I knew what was coming up next.

I knew what my next case had involved.

If this guy continued his pattern then . . .

Riley would be shot.

Panic nearly consumed me.

I needed a plan.

Desperately.

So what was I missing?

CHAPTER THIRTY-ONE

THERE WAS NO WAY I WAS GOING TO JUST SIT HERE WHILE Sierra was in jail and Sharon was suffering at the hands of a madman. Instead, I stood.

"Where are you going?" Riley asked.

"I am going to go talk to Freddy Mansfield again," I told him. "I want to see those letters he got from Bruce Patterson."

Riley rose also. "I'll go with you."

"I thought you had to work."

"I do. But there's no way I'm letting you do this alone."

Any other day, I might have argued with him. But, today, I knew I needed someone there with me. There was too much on the line for me to handle this alone.

An hour later, we arrived back at Freddy's house.

Just as before, I rang his doorbell and sounds of

supposed ghosts making their ghoulish noises echoed inside. A moment later, Freddy opened the creaky door.

"Twice in a week," he said, an almost *Twilight Zone*-like tone to his voice. "What a surprise."

"Can we come in?" I cut right to the chase.

"Of course." He extended his hand behind him.

We stepped inside just as a grandfather clock began clanging. I didn't bother to count the chimes.

I wasn't sure how Freddy managed to do it, but the inside of his house somehow smelled like an old castle. I saw a candle burning near the stairway, and I wondered if he'd purposely chosen that scent. Did they make candles in those scents?

I had much bigger issues to worry about right now, however.

I turned toward Freddy as we stood in the foyer.

"I assume you've probably heard on the news by now that there's a woman missing here in Norfolk." I studied his face, watching his reaction as my statement filled the air.

He didn't bother to look surprised. Instead, he nodded. "I heard. I'm sorry to hear someone has been taken. What can I do?"

"I'm glad you asked," I said. "You said that Bruce Patterson sent you some letters. Do you still have them?"

"Of course."

"Can we see them?"

Freddy narrowed his eyes, returning my scrutiny. "You really think that Bruce is behind this?"

I crossed my arms as I considered how much I should share. "I know he's been in town, and I know he's been watching me. So I'd say that, at this point, he's our best suspect."

He let my words wash over him a moment before slowly nodding and taking a step back. "Let me get you those letters then. Why don't you have a seat at the dining room table. I have a whole box that you're going to want to go through."

A whole box? I didn't have time to go through a whole box.

But I would scan everything that I could in hopes of finding a clue.

Two hours later, Riley and I had scanned almost all of the letters looking for a clue.

I found none.

That meant this had been another waste of time.

Most of the notes just talked about how deviously brilliant Milton Jones was. They almost sounded like the ramblings of a man who was losing his mind. Best I could tell, there was nothing in these letters I could use. In fact, everything he wrote was similar to what he'd posted on his blog.

"I guess this didn't help you." Freddy leaned against the doorframe with his arms crossed as he watched us.

"I wish I could say that it did," I started. "Unfortunately, these letters don't give me any better indication of where he might be than what I had before."

"So you know that he's in this area . . ." Freddy tapped his chin. "I'm trying to think about where I might be if I were Bruce."

Sadly, I'd tried to put myself in Bruce's shoes also. I didn't want to think that Freddy, Bruce, and I were all cut from the same cloth. But I had a better understanding of a killer's mind than I would like. Not because I was a killer. But because I'd dealt with so many of them.

But that wasn't exactly something I'd put on my résumé.

"Do you have any ideas?" I asked Freddy.

"He's going to be somewhere where he can't be seen that easily." Freddy stared off in the distance as he formulated his thoughts. "Probably somewhere where he can hide his vehicle as well. But he has to be close enough that he's keeping an eye on you. If I had to guess, he's probably no more than a mile or two from your place."

His words caused me to shiver. He was probably right. If Bruce was in town, he probably wasn't very far away. That would take away some of the thrill of seeing my demise and the downfall of my friends.

"There are a lot of houses and apartment complexes within a couple of miles of my place," I said as I tried to think through the logistics. "Though it does help me narrow it down, I'm afraid it's not enough."

"The apartment complexes will probably be too obvious," Freddy said. "He would have to park out in the open and pass a lot of people. I'm thinking that's probably not where he is. You can rule out some of the houses if you consider the fact that he's probably renting something. Either that or he broke in, but, if he's been in town for a while, we might have heard something if that was the case."

I nodded slowly. "Right. Maybe I should check all of the rental listings. I feel like the police would've probably already done that, though."

"And if that's the case, then maybe you're looking at somewhere that's been abandoned. A place where no one lives."

I slowly nodded. What he said sounded reasonable.

But how was I going to search all the abandoned buildings within a two-mile radius of my home?

CHAPTER THIRTY-TWO

WHEN RILEY AND I WERE DONE WITH FREDDY, WE HEADED back to our house. I wasn't sure if I should aimlessly wander around my area looking for abandoned buildings or use Google Maps or do something else more inventive.

What I really wanted was to hear how Sierra was doing. But I doubted that Chad would give me an update. He'd seemed so mad. My heart panged at the thought of it.

I hope that Riley was right and that Chad would get over it. But I knew there was a possibility that he would find me culpable for what happened to his wife, and I couldn't fault him for that.

I would blame myself if I were in his shoes.

In fact, I *did* blame myself.

Two of my friends' lives were falling apart, and it

was all because someone wanted revenge on *me*. How was I not guilty in this situation?

Riley and I parked on the street. As we started up the little sidewalk leading to our front door, I paused as movement at the house beside us caught my eye. My neighbor stepped from his front door.

A neighbor I hadn't seen for a month since he'd been on a cross-country tour for his talk radio talk show.

Bill McCormick.

Part of me felt too exhausted to deal with the man's antics and histrionic personality. But I couldn't walk by him without saying hello. Besides, I *did* want to know how he was doing.

He seemed to see me and Riley at the same time we spotted him, and a large smile stretched across his face. He strode our way.

"Riley and Gabby . . . just the people I wanted to see." Bill stopped in front of us, stared at us a moment, then pulled us both into an overwhelming bear hug.

"When did you get back?" I tried to suck in some deep breaths since my lungs had just been squeezed like a lemon during happy hour.

"Just this morning." His voice sounded jovial and animated—part of what made him interesting to listen to over the airwaves. He was a natural-born entertainer.

"I thought you were still another couple of weeks out." Riley put his hands in his pockets as he settled in for the conversation.

"I'll head back on the road after a short break. I actually need to have a root canal, so I had to cut a few dates from my tour. So here I am. It's just as well because I had some business to attend to here as well."

"You look good. Have you lost weight?" I almost hadn't recognized Bill for a brief moment. The man had been on the larger side at one time. He'd really thinned down recently.

"I have." He struck a model-like pose with one hand behind his head. "Looking good, right?"

He broke his pose and let out a long, infectious laugh that made him nearly double over.

"Absolutely." I grinned—I couldn't help myself. "Are things going well? Besides your tooth."

His laugh faded and he drew in a breath. "Honestly, I can't complain. My ratings are higher than ever, my books are doing well, and I've even been seeing somebody for the past few weeks." He gave us a wide-eyed, pointed look. "We'll see how that works out."

Not terribly long ago, Bill's ex-wife had been murdered, and he'd been blamed for it. With my help, he'd eventually been cleared, and the attention he'd received as a result had skyrocketed his career.

Talk about a blessing in disguise.

"Is everyone here doing well?" Bill asked.

I remembered everything that happened, and I didn't even know how to answer that without jumping into the entire explanation, which I didn't want to do.

"It's been an interesting few days, but we are hanging in," I finally decided to say. I'd explain everything else to him later. Right now, I didn't feel like chitchatting.

He nodded, unfettered by my unwillingness to share details. "Since I have you both here, I thought I should let you know that I'm putting my house up for sale. If there's anybody you know who's in the market, send them my way."

"You're putting your house up for sale?" Riley's eyebrows pushed together. "I thought you loved this place."

"I do. I have a better opportunity." Satisfaction lined his voice.

"What kind of opportunity is that?" I resisted the urge to look at my watch. But I was keenly aware of how time pressed down on me. Still, I did want to hear about Bill. The timing was just off.

"I can't share any details yet." He grinned. "But let's just say . . . I'm planning a bit of a surprise."

Great, Bill had a secret. I didn't think I could handle any more secrets right now.

"Listen, Bill. It's great to see you, but Gabby and I need to get inside to attend to a certain matter we've been working on." Riley put his hand on my lower back. "We will have you over for dinner sometime—if you're able to eat with your tooth issue. Otherwise, we'll try to catch up with you before you hit the road again."

"That sounds great." Bill waved his hand at us. "Later."

I couldn't wait to get away just to have a moment to think.

Bill could be a lot to handle, and I didn't want to play into his game of guessing what his big secret was. Not now, at least.

Riley and I stepped into our house, locking the door behind us.

To my surprise, Sir Watson didn't come to greet us like he always did.

Strange. Where was my canine friend?

Just as the question fluttered through my mind, a whine floated in the back bedroom, followed by a scratch at the door.

Had I accidentally left Watson locked in my bedroom? I *had* been distracted this morning.

But as I walked deeper into my house, I sensed a movement in the kitchen.

And when I looked up, I saw Bruce Patterson standing in the center of the room, a wild look in his eyes.

CHAPTER THIRTY-THREE

MY EYES WENT FROM BRUCE'S UNHINGED GAZE TO THE knife in his hands. Riley reached for my arm and pulled me back. We scooted closer to the front door.

Could we make a run for it?

Based on the man's body language, he was ready to spring. He'd be on us like a journalist fact-checking a politician.

"I don't want to hurt you." Bruce's trembling voice sounded hoarse.

Yeah, I had a lot of doubts about his statement—especially since he had a knife.

My eyes slid from his weapon back to his face.

His eyes look dilated, almost like he might be on something.

Danger practically crackled in the air.

How had this man even gotten inside?

I'd worry about that *after* I survived this situation.

Riley palmed the air. "If you want to talk, why don't you put the knife down?"

"I don't want to hurt you," he repeated. His eyes widened, still looking wild and irrational.

That's when I realized the knife Bruce held was mine. He'd pulled it right out of the block I kept on the kitchen counter.

"We don't want you to hurt us either." Riley's voice sounded calm and placating as he, no doubt, tried to defuse the situation. "But it's going to be really hard to talk while staring at that blade."

"I'm not putting it down." Bruce's voice quivered. "I might not want to hurt you, but I don't trust you either. I have to take precautions."

"Why are you here?" My mind raced.

Would we be his next victims?

This seemed too random. Something about this situation didn't fit.

I couldn't pinpoint what exactly.

I glanced around, searching for something to defend myself with. Maybe I could grab the glass lamp from the table beside me. That would slow Bruce down some.

Or maybe Bill would spot us through the window and call the police.

It was doubtful.

But there still had to be *something* we could do. I

couldn't just stand here defenseless. Nor could I let this man hurt someone else I loved—Riley.

I suppose I should be thankful Bruce didn't have a gun and that he hadn't come to act out that terrible, gut-wrenching moment from my past.

Bruce still gripped the knife. "I came here to thank you."

"Thank us?" Riley repeated.

"Not you." Bruce nodded at me. "Her."

"Why would you want to thank me?" This conversation was making less sense all the time.

Bruce looked at me with his beady gaze. "Because you killed Milton Jones."

"You want to . . . thank me for what?" I stumbled over my words, certain I hadn't heard Bruce correctly. He was making absolutely no sense.

"That's right," Bruce continued. "Thanks to you, an evil man died. He finally got the justice he deserved, even though I personally believe he should have suffered more. But, at least, he doesn't have the privilege of living."

My head wobbled, just a little. I had no idea what was going on here. I'd assumed this man *loved* Milton Jones. From the sound of it, Bruce was happy Milton was dead.

Was that because it was easier to follow in the man's footsteps if Milton wasn't around to stop him?

My throat tightened.

That was the only thing that made sense.

"You said thank you." Riley's voice sounded tight with unmasked tension. "Is that all you wanted?"

"Maybe. I've been trying to catch Gabby since I arrived in town so I could tell you this. But I could tell you were spooked. The timing wasn't right."

This conversation wasn't going at all the way I thought it would. I still had so many questions.

I licked my lips before asking, "Why did you come into town, Bruce?"

"It's like I said. To say thank you."

He may have been thanking us, but it was hard to hear anything beyond the sight of that knife he held.

"And that's all?" Riley kept his steady gaze on the man.

"Yes. Why else do you think I would be here?" What sounded like earnest surprise stretched through the man's voice.

"That's what we've been trying to figure out," I said. "We came home to find you in our kitchen holding a knife. That's rather an odd way of saying thank you, don't you think?"

"I didn't mean . . . I just had to do what I came here to do."

"Did you have something to do with Sharon Wilkinson's disappearance?"

Bruce nearly snorted. "Why would I have anything to do with that woman's disappearance?"

The man's words sounded surprisingly genuine. "Because you're following in Milton Jones's footsteps."

"Why would I do that?" Bruce looked at us as if totally perplexed as to where this conversation was going.

"Because you're obsessed with him," Riley said, a hint of irritation in his voice. "We've seen all your letters. We've talked to people who had encounters with you."

"You have it all wrong," Bruce said. "The only reason I am obsessed with Milton Jones is because he killed somebody I care about. I'm glad that Milton is dead."

CHAPTER THIRTY-FOUR

I WAS CERTAIN THAT I HADN'T HEARD BRUCE CORRECTLY.
"Come again?"

"That man killed my Carrie," he growled.

"Carrie Mills?" Riley's breath hitched.

Bruce's eyes lit up when he heard Carrie's full name.
"Yes, Carrie Mills. My Carrie."

"How are you and Carrie connected?" I asked, trying
to put the pieces together.

"I was her boyfriend."

Riley straightened ever so slightly. "But Carrie Mills
was dating Dan Larkins."

"She was—that's what everybody thought, at least.
But the two of us were seeing each other on the side. She
was going to break up with Dan, going to leave him
for me."

Riley shook his head as if something about Bruce's story didn't compute.

He obviously knew more about this than I did. He'd dedicated years of his life to prosecuting Milton and knew each of the victim's families because of that.

"If that was true, your name would have come up during the investigation," Riley said. "You would have been a suspect."

"We kept everything secret." Bruce dropped his voice. "I didn't realize we'd done such a good job keeping things on the down low, but we did. Nobody knew. Nobody but me and Carrie."

"How was that even possible?" Riley asked. "The police extensively questioned people in connection with the case. It seems your name would have come up at some point."

"Easy. Carrie lived out in the country. Nobody was ever around. I could come and go, and no one ever saw me." A touch of wistfulness entered his voice.

"Carrie was Milton's fourth victim?" He'd murdered thirteen women all together during his reign of terror. I tried to remember how Carrie fit.

"That's right." Bruce's expression hardened again. "My life hasn't been the same since then. I just can't seem to get a grip."

The knife trembled in his hands, and I tried to figure out what his game plan was. To hurt us? Since he was holding a knife, that made the most sense.

"I saw the letters that you sent Freddy Mansfield," I started. "None of them said anything about your girlfriend."

"I didn't think that I could trust him with that information," Bruce said.

"But you just told us, and we didn't even have to push you to reveal it. I don't understand . . ."

He swallowed hard, and his eyes latched onto mine. "It's because you're my hero. Of *course*, I'll share it with you. You're the person who made all of this right."

I sucked in a breath. "Nobody else knows about you and Carrie besides the three of us?"

"That's right. I don't want people to know. Our relationship won't seem as special or real if I start telling people about it."

I hated to admit it, but his words were almost sweet. I couldn't let that thought muddy my perception of the man, though.

"You've spent all these years thinking about her?" Obviously, the man wasn't over her death. He was still obsessing over it. That was a lot of time for bitterness and vengeance to build in him.

I wasn't sure exactly when Carrie had died, but Riley had been in Virginia for five years. Based on that fact, I was going to guess that Carrie had been dead for at least seven or eight.

"You don't ever get over losing the love of your life."

Bruce's lips twisted, as if his emotions were beginning to rise.

As his words hung in the air, I remembered how I had almost lost the love of my life.

If Bruce told the truth—that he wasn't the killer—then the real madman could still be out there, waiting to shoot Riley in the head at the first opportunity.

Riley's body went tense again as he nudged himself in front of me. Something about what Bruce said must have raised a red flag.

"What are you going to do now?" Riley eyed Bruce cautiously. "You told Gabby thank you."

Riley sounded about as certain as I felt. This guy's story *could* check out. But that didn't mean he wasn't unhinged. It also didn't mean that he wasn't behind some of these crimes that had recently happened.

Bruce shrugged. "I guess I'll head back to California."

There was no way I could let this conversation end without going back to the most important question.

"I need to ask you this again, Bruce. Did you grab my friend Sharon?" My voice waivered as the words left my lips. But he'd obviously known who she was. Was that because he was behind her disappearance? Or had he heard her name on the news?

Bruce nearly snorted again. The motion caused one of his stringy hairs to fall in his eyes. "Like I said, why would I do that? I don't want to hurt other people the way that Milton hurt me."

"You understand why it might seem suspicious that you appeared when you did, right?"

"What do you mean?" He squinted, looking honestly confused.

I supposed I was going to have to spell this out if it was going to make any sense.

"I just . . . I need to find my friend. Do you know where she is?"

"Why would I know?" He scratched his head using his free hand.

I decided to try a different tactic. "Because you're observant, Bruce. You've been around. Maybe you've seen something."

"I haven't seen *anything*," he said quickly.

I tilted my head. "Are you sure about that?"

Bruce held his knife out farther. He was getting defensive, I realized. I couldn't push him too hard or I might regret it.

"Of course, I'm sure!" His voice contained more of a hard edge now.

Riley took a step closer as the tension in the room escalated. "Why don't we all head down to the police station so that you can tell them what you just told us?

Or if you're not comfortable with that, I can call them and they'll come here."

"I don't want to talk to no police!" Bruce's voice rose with every syllable.

My theory was confirmed. This man was becoming more unhinged. This wasn't good.

Sir Watson barked in the background as if he sensed the situation was beginning to heighten.

"You said you didn't do anything wrong," I continued, my voice mirroring Riley's calm tone. "The police will understand."

I didn't believe my words 100 percent. Mostly, I didn't want this guy to slip away, and I could feel that he was going to. I had to convince him to talk more.

Almost as if Bruce had read my thoughts, he stepped toward the back door.

His gaze darted from me to Riley then back again.

Clearly, he was trying to get a read on the situation. Had he been spooked?

The next instant, he dropped the knife and darted outside.

CHAPTER THIRTY-FIVE

RILEY AND I TOOK OFF AFTER BRUCE.

But the man ran with surprising focus.

By the time we reached the back yard, Bruce had already jumped the front fence and was racing down the sidewalk.

I had no idea what Riley and I would do if we caught him. I only knew I couldn't let him get away.

Maybe he was innocent.

But maybe he *wasn't*.

And if he wasn't innocent, then he could be my one chance of finding Sharon and clearing Sierra.

My legs burned as I pushed myself down the sidewalk.

Only three blocks ahead was a city park.

A park where little kids liked to play.

I didn't want this guy to make it that far. Too many innocent people had already been in danger.

Yet I couldn't simply let him escape either.

Our best bet was to catch him before he reached the park.

Riley moved faster than I did. But Bruce still had too much of a head start.

He turned the corner, disappearing from sight.

Just as we rounded the turn, a noise cut through the air.

Gunfire.

I dove toward Riley and tackled him to the ground.

I couldn't let a bullet pierce his body again.

Not if I could do something to stop it.

My heart pounded in my ears with such force I could hardly hear.

All I could think about was Riley.

If something happened to him.

If it was my fault.

He shifted beneath me, letting out a soft groan.

In my rush to save him, maybe I shouldn't have thrown him down on concrete. But I'd take that to a bullet piercing his skin.

"Are you okay?" I rushed, trying to keep the panic from my voice.

As he shifted again, I slid to the sidewalk. His gaze met mine, and I saw that his face was unharmed except for a little mud on his cheek. We weren't out of danger yet.

But I was going to treasure this moment.

"I'm fine." Riley sounded breathless. "You?"

I nodded and leaned down to plant a quick kiss on his lips. "I'm fine."

We exchanged a look, another one of those that said a thousand words without saying anything aloud.

But the moment was cut short as another crack of gunfire sliced through the air.

This was far from over.

Remaining on the ground, I glanced around.

Bruce was nowhere to be seen.

But, across the street, a twenty-something woman climbed from her car.

Air Pods were in her ears.

She had no idea what was going on, did she? Had no idea bullets were being fired nearby.

"Get down!" I yelled.

If she couldn't hear the bullets, what made me think that she was going to hear me?

But, by God's grace, she glanced at me.

When she saw Riley and me on the ground, her eyes widened.

I motioned for her to get down and then made a

finger gun with my hands. As I did, she quickly scrambled behind her car.

Another shot rang out.

Where was the gunman?

I looked around again, but I didn't see him anywhere. He couldn't be too far away. And who was his target?

Sirens sounded in the distance.

Help was on the way.

I planned on staying right here until help arrived.

Because if *I* got up, *Riley* was going to get up.

I wasn't going to risk nearly losing him again.

CHAPTER THIRTY-SIX

As police surrounded the area, the gunshots ceased.

The shooter must have fled.

No doubt, units from all over the area were searching for him.

When several minutes passed with no incidents, I raised my head and searched for any sign of Bruce.

I saw nothing . . . except an ambulance pulling up the next street over.

What had happened? Had an innocent bystander been hurt?

The woman across the street scurried into her house. As she did, Riley and I stood. As we brushed the dirt from our clothes, a police sedan stopped beside us.

Detective Adams. He motioned for us to climb into the back of his car.

We did.

"You two look rough." Adams grimaced as he glanced back at us. "Do you know anything about Bruce Patterson being shot the next street over?"

I squeezed my eyes shut. It was as I feared.

Bruce had been hurt.

"Is he okay?" Was he dead?

"He's in critical condition. Shot in the chest. Paramedics are taking him to the hospital now." Adams turned just enough to stare at me through his droopy eyelids. "Care to explain?"

I filled him in on what happened, all the way to when gunshots had pierced the air.

Adams's expression morphed from curious to apprehensive. "Do you think Bruce has Sharon?"

"I'm not sure. He said he didn't. Part of me believes him. But the other part of me thinks the man wasn't in his right frame of mind. He was my one hope of finding some answers."

"But if he's not the one behind this . . ." Detective Adams's voice trailed.

I knew exactly what he was getting at.

If Bruce wasn't responsible, then who was?

That meant that the killer was still out there.

And that meant we didn't have any other leads to help point us to the person behind this.

We were back to square one.

And that was unacceptable.

Adams took our statements and then offered to drop us off at our house. We decided to walk instead.

As we began to pace down the sidewalk, I murmured, "What now?"

This wasn't the way I'd expected things to go.

Riley shook his head, almost looking defeated. And he wasn't the defeated type.

"I'm not sure," he finally murmured. "Maybe we should go back to the house and regroup."

I nodded somberly and started back around the block to our place. As I did, one of our neighbors who lived three houses down waved hello to us.

Mr. Nelson, a widower, was retired from the railroad, and he loved to keep an eye on everyone on our street. He used gardening as an excuse to do so.

He was a nice man who loved finding someone to talk to. Usually, that was fine—unless I was dealing with a ticking time bomb.

Like now.

"Quite a commotion going on over there," Mr. Nelson said. "In all my years living here, I've seen a lot of things. But it's been a long time since I've heard gunshots in broad daylight."

I nodded, wishing he'd just been imagining things. But he hadn't been. "I know. Hopefully, this will all be over soon."

"Did I hear that your neighbor is putting his house on the market?" He leaned on his rake, looking like he had all the time in the world.

I blinked, feeling slightly stupefied. "Bill? I'm surprised you have already heard, especially since he just got back into town."

Mr. Nelson squinted. "Just got back into town? I saw him three days ago."

My back muscles tightened. "Are you sure? Bill specifically told me he just got back today."

"I'm quite certain. I saw him right before I left to play bridge, and I play bridge every Friday."

Why would Bill have lied to me about being in town?

And if Mr. Nelson had seen him three days ago . . . that meant that Bill had been back here right around the time this crime spree started.

Bill knew enough about me to know my weaknesses. To know about my love of music. To know about the crimes I'd solved.

Was that a coincidence?

I wanted to think that it was.

But Bill had also hinted he had a secret. What if . . .

I shook my head. I didn't want my thoughts to go there. But I couldn't seem to stop them.

What if Bill was behind this?

If that was the case, how would I ever prove it?

CHAPTER THIRTY-SEVEN

RILEY AND I GOT BACK INTO OUR HOUSE. I HESITATED before going inside. Images of finding Bruce there earlier filled my mind.

Even though I knew he wouldn't be there, my back muscles tightened anyway.

"Let me check things out first," Riley murmured, seeming to read my thoughts.

Thank goodness.

He returned a few minutes later and deemed the place clear.

Afterward, we let Sir Watson out before sitting at the kitchen table. I shared my theory about Bill with him, and Riley listened. He hadn't denied it was a possibility that Bill could be behind these crimes.

What other reason did Bill have for lying?

I glanced out the back window, and I saw Bill's car

parked near his garage. I had the perfect angle to see from my seat.

Had Bill somehow heard what was happening with Bruce in my kitchen? What if he'd seen Bruce run from my back door? When that happened, Bill could have cut over a few streets in an effort to stop Bruce. Maybe he feared that Bruce knew something that could implicate him.

That might be a stretch. But I'd be foolish if I didn't examine every possibility.

"What are you thinking?" Riley rose and began fixing us some coffee.

I really could use something to give me a mental boost right now. As I listened to the pot gurgling in the background, I began to salivate for a taste of the bitter caffeine laced with some sugar and milk.

I leaned back and rubbed a hand over my eyes. "I don't know. My thoughts are muddled. I mean, let's say my theory is right. What would Bill's motivation be?"

Riley sighed. "I think whoever's behind these crimes has a personal vendetta against you, Gabby. Maybe someone just wants to get the ultimate revenge on you."

I chewed on his words a moment. "If Bill was in town three days ago, he'd have the opportunity. And let's say you're right. That would give him motive. So then we would have to ask ourselves if Bill had the means to do any of these things."

"I think the guy's pretty smart and can probably do

whatever he sets his mind to do. Plus, he has a lot of followers. I'm sure he could have talked one of them into helping him out." Riley rose to pour us the coffee, fixed mine with all my extras, and then brought the two mugs back to the table for us.

Before he sat down, something flew into the back door.

I suppressed a scream and jumped from my seat.

Instantly, I searched for my purse.

For the gun there.

Then I saw Sir Watson appear in the little glass pane.

When the canine saw me, he barked, clearly letting me know he wanted to come inside.

I released my breath, a small laugh escaping with it.

It was just my dog. Of course.

But it would be a long time before I lost my jumpiness. I kept expecting another surprise to hit me at any minute. The feeling was terrible.

That wasn't the kind of surprise I liked.

No, it was a horrible kind of surprise—like having your heart ripped out of your chest in that Indiana Jones movie.

I drew in a deep breath and got back to the subject. "So, if it is Bill, what do we do? Do we confront him? Do we tell the police?"

Riley shook his head and took a long sip of his coffee before answering. "We don't confront him. Besides, we have no evidence. I say what we do right now is we watch Bill and keep our eyes on him."

I nodded in agreement with his assessment.

Just then, my phone buzzed. I glanced at the screen and saw I had a message from an unknown number.

As I read the words, that sinking feeling returned to my gut.

Do I need to spell it out for you? Answers are under your nose. You are making this no fun. Take Me Back.

An audio file was beneath it. As I clicked on it, the strands of the Monkees' "Homecoming Queen" began to play.

CHAPTER THIRTY-EIGHT

"'HOMECOMING QUEEN'?" I ASKED RILEY.

"Why would he send that song? All the other messages have been song titles. Sending a song doesn't match the rest."

I sighed, wishing this all made sense. "I have no idea. This is becoming more confusing all the time. Although, the second part of this message might be a song. 'Take Me Back'?"

Riley nodded. "As a matter of fact, I think Andraé Crouch sang a song with that title."

"Maybe 'back' is significant—like he's going back in time or on a gruesome stroll down memory lane?"

"Maybe." Riley shrugged.

I pulled up the lyrics to "Homecoming Queen" on my phone so I could read them, hoping something different would hit me.

And it didn't.

Not at first, at least.

But then I realized that there *was* a line about sleepy Jean. I sat up straighter and showed Riley my screen. "That's it!"

"What?" He leaned closer.

"Sleepy Jean," I told him. "Bill's ex-wife was named Emma Jean."

Riley narrowed his eyes. "Do you think Bill sent us this to implicate himself?"

I nibbled on my bottom lip. "You're right. That wouldn't make any sense, would it?"

"This guy is toying with you, Gabby."

I frowned as I nodded. "I think he's enjoying himself a little bit too much."

"I agree."

"Does this mean the answers are under my nose? He's almost making it sound like there's something I'm missing."

"I don't know. But we need to figure this out."

As he said the words, I glanced out my window and saw Bill climbing into his car. "I wonder where he's going . . ."

Without saying anything, Riley and I rose.

We needed to follow Bill and keep him in our sights.

Riley drove. That was a good thing because I could hardly breathe.

Where was Bill going?

He'd taken a few turns, but we finally had him in our sights again. He was headed toward the outskirts of downtown Norfolk.

Bill had always seemed a little batty, but I didn't know if I could see him as being a killer.

Then again, I really couldn't see anybody I considered a friend as a killer.

My head pounded at the thought.

I craned my neck, trying to do a mind meld with Bill. Not really. But I did have a lot of questions for him.

"Where in the world is he going?" I murmured.

"This is Bill. Who knows? Is there a political rally anywhere downtown?"

"Not that I know of."

"He could just be grabbing lunch, for all we know."

"But if we keep an eye on him, maybe he'll do something that gives us a clue."

"We can only hope."

I really hoped we weren't wasting our time again. I knew time was a precious commodity, especially because Sharon was being kept at the hands of this killer.

I needed to call Clarice again. Needed to check on her and see how she was doing, how she was holding up through all of this.

Bill turned again.

I realized that we were headed toward our old neighborhood.

Just what was he up to?

We kept following and watched as Bill pulled into the parking lot behind The Grounds. Did he think the place had opened back up?

Because he knew that Sharon was missing.

It seemed like an odd choice.

Riley waited until he got out and stepped around the corner of the building before finding a parking space nearby.

We parked and quietly hurried behind him, trying not to lose sight of him.

Bill bypassed The Grounds and crossed the street instead.

Just what was he up to?

Based on the way he looked around, he almost seemed paranoid.

Maybe he *was* our guy.

We were about to find out.

CHAPTER THIRTY-NINE

I CONTINUED TO WATCH AS BILL CROSSED THE STREET AND paused on the sidewalk where our old apartment complex used to stand.

He remained there with his hands on his hips as he looked at the new structure being built.

"What in the world is he doing?" I whispered to Riley.

"I have no idea. His actions aren't making much sense to me now."

I gripped Riley's arm as we peered at Bill. "I think we just need to talk to him."

"I agree." Riley gave an affirmative nod. "We don't have any time to waste."

We charged across the street, choosing not to announce our presence. I didn't want to give Bill the opportunity to run or think of a quick excuse. I was doing him a favor by questioning him first instead of calling the police first.

I hoped I didn't regret it.

I approached Bill on one side and Riley took the other. Our neighbor's eyes widened when he turned and saw us standing there.

"Gabby? Riley? I wasn't expecting to see you two here." He let out a nervous laugh.

I didn't want to pretend like nothing was wrong, so I didn't waste any time with my questions. "What's going on, Bill? What are you up to?"

As soon as I asked the question, a thin sheen of sweat seemed to cover his face. "What do you mean? What makes you think I'm up to something?"

I narrowed my eyes, putting on my don't-mess-with-me persona. "I know that you haven't been telling us the truth. You've been in town for at least four days. You lied and told us you'd just gotten back today."

The beads of sweat across his skin seemed to triple.

"I don't know what you're talking about." He let out another nervous laugh.

"We don't have any time for games." Riley put his hands on his hips. "What are you up to?"

Bill's eyes widened as realization seemed to dawn on him. "Wait . . . you don't think that I'm up to something illegal, do you?"

"All we know is that the person behind these crimes is someone that Gabby knows," Riley said. "At this point, no suspects are off the table, no matter how much we like them or consider them a friend."

Bill shook his head, lifting his hands in the air. "I would never do anything to hurt Gabby. You've got to know that. I think of you two as family."

"Did you come into town four days ago?" I questioned.

"I did," he stated as a matter of fact. "But not for the reasons that you're thinking."

I didn't try to hide my scowl. "The fact that you lied to us doesn't bode well."

He shook his head a little too quickly, his nerves obviously getting the best of him. "Slow your roll and let me explain. It's not what you think."

I held my breath as I waited for Bill to start.

His talk show voice disappeared as he said, "I bought this land, and I'm building this house."

I blinked, not sure if I'd heard him correctly. "What?"

He nodded. "It's true. I've done pretty well for myself, and I wanted to do something that would remind me of my roots. When I heard this property was going up for sale, I knew it would be perfect. I wanted to build a house similar to the Victorian where we used to live."

I looked at the structure being built, and shock coursed through me. "I had no idea."

"*This* was your secret?" Disbelief stretched through Riley's voice.

Bill nodded. "Once the house was finished, I wanted to have you guys over so you could see it. I'm *really* excited about this."

I couldn't deny he sounded thrilled. But . . . "Why did you lie about when you got into town?"

"I came into town early because I had to answer some questions for the contractor—and I really do need a root canal also. But if I told you about the contractor, then you would have realized what I was doing. I wanted this to be a surprise. I had this big reveal planned in my head involving balloons and a slide show and maybe some miniature horses."

I didn't ask how the horses fit in.

"How did we not see you?" Riley asked. "You live beside us."

"I've been working late hours and sleeping in my office at the studio," Bill said. "I only came home when I knew you two were gone. I know it sounds extreme, but I had high hopes of how this would go. Not like this. Did I mention the miniature horses?"

"Wow . . ." I shook my head as I stared up at the building. "This is unexpected. I'm sorry we ruined your surprise."

"I'd take you on a tour, but it's not safe right now.

Plus, we've been delayed because of some permit issues. But you're going to be amazed when you see the inside. I tried to re-create the original structure the best I could so it would be like it was when we all lived there."

Finally, some of the tension seemed to leave Riley, and he shook his head. "That's really exciting, Bill. Congratulations."

Bill's face beamed. "The staircase is even in the same place. It won't be four separate apartments, but the basic layout is going to be the same."

"I can't wait to see it," I said.

But as much as I wanted to hear about this, I had other things on my mind right now. Other things like finding Sharon.

Despite that, Bill then continued to tell me details I wasn't prepared to hear.

"I was going to add a balcony where your old fire escape used to be," Bill said. "But there's only a view of the dumpster back there. Instead, I decided at the last minute to move it to off the bedroom. There's a wonderful view of downtown Norfolk from there."

He continued on and on and on.

Finally, Riley and I were able to slip away.

But for the second time today, we were back at square one.

And that was one place I hated to be.

CHAPTER FORTY

"WHAT ARE YOU THINKING?" RILEY ASKED AS WE WALKED away from Bill and back toward our car.

"I'm thinking of one of the earlier clues this guy sent. 'Take Me Back.'"

"What do you think it means?"

I half-frowned, half-nibbled on the side of my lip before answering. "For me, my crime solving spree began at the home of the Cunninghams. That's where I was picking that piece of skull out of the wall, and I found the gun that the police missed, and then the house was set on fire."

Riley cast a quick glance my way as we reached the car and climbed inside. "Do you want to go see it again?"

I shrugged, torn between turning every stone and feeling like I was acting out of desperation. As I pulled my seatbelt on, I said, "I know it's a long shot. But I've got to do something. It seems like it's worth checking out at least."

"I agree." He put the car in Drive, and, without any more questions, we took off toward the expensive Virginia Beach neighborhood where that first crime had occurred.

It felt like ages ago when I'd last been here. Back then, I was so green and naïve—at least, in some ways.

But I vividly remembered how I'd been trying to find my place in the world. To find my mission in life.

I felt like I'd started to find it that day.

It was too bad I'd almost lost my life several times since discovering that, however.

I ignored the nerves that started to seep into me as we headed down the road. I hadn't expected to feel this nervous. But I hadn't been back to this house in a long time. My last memories there weren't great ones, to say the least.

"So, Bill bought the old place," Riley said as the suburbs blurred past our windows. Darkness was falling, making everything look appropriately gray around us.

I shook my head. "I can't believe it. There were a lot of things I'd expected to discover when we followed Bill. But his secret was nothing I'd ever anticipated."

"That's the way life works sometimes, isn't it? What we think is going to be a curveball ends up being a blessing, and what we think is going to be a blessing . . ."

I couldn't argue with that assessment.

"I hope Bill is happy." Riley gripped the steering wheel. "It *will* be nice to see that old place restored. Or should I say to watch it rise from the ashes."

"Speaking of which . . ." I glanced at my phone. "I'm pretty sure I got a text from my father earlier about Tim."

"What about him?"

I scrolled through my messages until I found the one I was looking for. My eyes widened as I read the words. "Tim is being released early."

"How early?"

I frowned. "Yesterday."

"What? I'm surprised he didn't call anyone to pick him up."

"I hope that doesn't mean he called one of his new friends to pick him up." I knew what that would mean —trouble.

My mom used to say watch out who you hang out with because you'll eventually become like them. I used to argue with her that her assessment wasn't true. But it was.

If Tim started hanging out with people who were into drugs, he was going to fall right back into that life-style. I prayed that didn't happen.

"I wish the best for him," Riley said. "I guess this means he can be at your dad's wedding."

"It looks like he got out just in time. But I really hope he doesn't ruin Dad and Teddi's big day." I could totally see it happening. I didn't want to picture it, but how could I not?

Just then, we pulled up to the Cunningham house. Which was no longer the Cunningham house. The place was still stately, built in one of the more affluent, spacious neighborhoods. The brick-covered structure made it clear that whoever lived inside was important.

That's what Michael Cunningham had thought also.

Now he was dead. Someone had killed him in my old apartment while I'd been investigating the murder of the man's wife.

I licked my lips and braced myself for the upcoming conversation.

A woman close to my age answered the door only a few seconds after I rang the bell. She had a toddler on her hip, and more kids chattered in the background. The scent of roast beef floated through the air.

Immediately, I regretted disturbing them. What did I expect to find here?

I had no idea, but I'd hoped something would jump out at me.

The last thing I wanted was to pull this woman and her little family into my mess. It seemed like I had a knack for doing that.

"Can I help you?" She bounced her little boy in her arms.

As soon as I saw her doing that, my thoughts rushed back to Sierra. She should be able to hold her son and bounce him in her arms also.

Maybe I should go see her. But would Sierra even want to talk to me? Or did she feel the same way Chad did?

I frowned.

"I know this is going to sound strange." Riley took the lead. "I'm Riley, and this is my wife, Gabby. We helped to renovate this house several years ago after a fire here. We got to talking, and we wondered if you would ever consider selling this place. We know it's a long shot but . . . we have a lot of memories here."

Wow, Riley had come a long way when it came to investigating. He'd come up with that excuse on his own.

"I'm Sarah. And I've got to honestly say I have no desire to move." Sarah let out a little laugh. "It's too much work, especially with little kids."

"You sound busy," Riley said.

"I am." She glanced over her shoulder as a child giggled in another room before she turned back to us and smiled. "But I'm not complaining."

"This is a great house," Riley said. "If you don't mind me asking, how long ago did you move in?"

"Three years. This sat on the market for quite a while. I guess this place has some type of morbid history."

So she didn't know. Or did Sarah not want to say it out loud?

Me? I would have been all over the internet trying to find out the history of any home I'd bought. As a matter of fact, I'd done that with the house where Riley and I now lived.

Its history was squeaky clean, though, so I had no worries about some type of bad history seeping into the walls. Not that I believed in that kind of stuff.

"It's probably just as well," I piped in. "We'll keep looking and waiting for some other houses in this neighborhood to go on the market. But . . . I have heard that there's been some break-ins in this area. Is it still safe here?"

The smile slipped from her face, and she shrugged. "I haven't heard anything."

"Good," I jumped in. "That's really good. That means you haven't seen anything either?"

She shook her head. "Believe me, I'm home with these kids all day while my husband works. I haven't seen anything of note—unless you count a deer I spotted across the street last week. That's about as strange as it gets around here."

"I understand," I said. "We're sorry to bug you. We just thought it couldn't hurt to ask, right?"

"No, that's okay. It's no worry at all." She pointed behind her. "But I do need to go check on dinner."

"Thank you again," Riley called.

I paused before walking away. "Just one more thing. What's your last name, if you don't mind me asking? You seem familiar to me."

She didn't really seem familiar. I only wanted more information.

"Patagonia. Why?"

The blood drained from my face. "I hope this doesn't sound insensitive, but did you have a death in the family this week?"

Her expression turned terse. "As a matter of fact, we did. My husband's brother was killed while he was out jogging. Why are you asking?"

I glanced at Riley.

I almost couldn't bear telling her the truth.

The person behind this had planted another clue for me.

He'd killed an innocent man, just so I could live this moment.

CHAPTER FORTY-ONE

"WHAT NEXT?" RILEY TURNED TO ME AS WE DROVE AWAY from the house.

"This guy is even sicker than I thought." My voice sounded surprisingly thin, surprisingly frail. "He killed that man just to prove a connection between my first case with Michael Cunningham and now."

Riley's jaw stiffened. "I know. I don't like this."

I stared out the window at the gray landscape around me, landscape dotted with streetlights that began to pop on in the early twilight. "What else could he mean when he said take me back?"

"Good question," Riley said. "Do you think he could be talking about your childhood home?"

"Maybe. But who knows who owns that at this point? My gut is telling me that's not it." I sucked in a breath. "Wait. What if it's the house that Bill is building?"

"Our old place? The one we were just at?"

"Bear with me because I know this sounds crazy." A surge of adrenaline rushed through me, revitalizing my lagging thoughts. "Just think about it for a minute. That house is where it all goes back to. That's where we all met. That's where I was living. That's where my business was based out of."

"Don't you think we would have noticed something when we were there earlier?"

"It's not like we've been watching the place. The walls are up so who knows what's lurking behind them. Besides, from that location, this guy would have had a clear view of The Grounds. He could have watched us investigate. Watched us talking to Sharon. It's the perfect location."

Riley shrugged. "I suppose it's worth a shot. At this point, I'm pretty much game for anything. Do you think we should call the police first?"

I nibbled on my bottom lip for a minute. "I would say yes, but we've had so many leads that haven't paid off yet. I'm not sure we want to get the police involved until we know something for sure."

"So, we go inside and if we see any sign of anything suspicious, we call the police right then," Riley clarified. "Deal?"

"It's a deal," I told him.

Another rumble of nerves went through me. I'd been wrong so many times so far. Who was to say I wasn't going to be wrong again right now? But the only way I was going to feel defeated was if I didn't do anything at all.

I couldn't just sit back. I had to find Sharon. I had to free Sierra.

What was I missing?

I remembered that little boy's description of someone who looked like Riley.

I remembered the man from the video who'd come into The Grounds. I could see where somebody of his height and stature might resemble Riley, especially if you weren't looking at any of the details.

I remembered all the planning this person had put into reenacting all these crimes and making me miserable.

That formed a picture in my mind of what kind of person we were dealing with. Someone meticulous. Obsessive. Smart.

But who?

What if this person wasn't working with somebody? Now that we'd eliminated Bruce, we could say with a good measure of certainty that this guy was a lone wolf. Those earlier song titles using "us" and "we" were most likely meant to throw me off.

But it was obviously somebody who'd done a lot of research on me. I even had a feeling it was someone I'd talked to extensively before. Maybe he was even in my circle.

I shook my head. I'd considered Parker and Adams. But I really didn't think they were guilty. And I *knew* with absolute certainty that Riley wasn't guilty.

Bill? I didn't want to think he was behind this. But if we found any evidence at his house, he might go back on my suspect list.

We pulled up to the coffeehouse, and Riley put the car in Park.

I stared at the building across the street.

Here went nothing.

As I stepped into the house, my flashlight aimed at the floor, I glanced around. Memories flooded me.

So much of my life had been spent here. So much of the formative time while I'd really figured out who I was.

To my left would have been Sierra's old apartment, where she liked to burn incense and listen to the sound of whales in the ocean. I secretly thought the incense was to cover up the scent of her cats. She could never say no to taking in a stray.

To my right was Bill's old place.

If I walked up the grand staircase, Riley's place would

have been on my left, and I'd lived on the right. The third floor was where Mrs. Mystery had lived. The octogenarian wrote crime novels, and her love of privacy shrouded her in intrigue as well. She'd moved to Florida not long ago.

I'd met Riley for the first time in the parking lot outside this place. Sierra and I had been attempting to rescue a stray parrot. Riley and I still had that parrot—aptly named Lucky—in our house. I had a feeling that bird would outlive us.

So many memories.

Right now, rooms had been laid out and drywall covered the wood constructs. More progress had been made inside than I'd assumed.

I could tell that construction workers had been here. Stray bottles as well as candy bar wrappers littered the floor.

But nothing that raised any red flags.

It was already getting dark outside, which made being in this house even creepier than it needed to be.

"You really think there's a place to hide someone in here?" I asked Riley.

"The walls are up, so we should probably check closets and bathrooms, just to be sure." Riley shone his flashlight around the perimeter. "But let's stick together."

I liked that idea. I scooted closer to him, finding immense comfort in his presence.

We headed left first, toward the area where Sierra had once lived.

Riley opened a few doors, but nothing was inside.

We continued in a clockwise rotation around the first floor. There was no sign of Sharon or of anybody else being in here recently other than construction workers.

Why did I have a feeling this might all turn out to be nothing again?

That seemed to be a pattern lately.

"Should we go to the second floor?" Riley shone his light up the stairs.

For some reason, I shuddered. But, still, I said, "I think we should."

Riley reached his hand out, and I slipped my fingers into his.

Together, we walked up the staircase and paused at the top. The second level wasn't nearly as open as the first. A hallway turned on either side of us with various rooms behind doorways.

"I think we should check where your apartment used to be located first," Riley said.

Just as he said the words, I heard something in the distance.

Was that movement?

Or was I hearing things?

But Riley froze also.

He'd heard it too, hadn't he?

The sound had come from the very area where my apartment used to be.

I supposed that would be poetic justice. At least, it would be for a killer bent on revenge.

"Is this the part where we need to call the police?" I asked Riley.

"Yes." He reached for the phone in his pocket.

But before he could dial, he froze. His eyes glazed as he stared at me. Then he sank to the floor.

"Riley?" I reached for him, concern pulsing through me.

What in the world was going on?

Before I could check his pulse, something sharp pricked my neck.

I'd just been shot with some type of needle.

A sedative?

That was my last thought before everything around me went black.

CHAPTER FORTY-TWO

I OPENED MY EYES, AND THE FIRST THING I NOTICED WAS MY throbbing headache.

Everything was blurry around me, and my thoughts were muddled.

What happened?

I blinked several times, hoping my vision would clear.

It didn't.

I tried to touch my neck where I'd felt that prick right before everything went black.

But I couldn't.

My hands wouldn't move. They were . . . tied behind me. To the chair where I sat.

My lungs seized as reality settled on me even more harshly.

Someone had made Riley pass out. And then me. And now I was tied up.

I blinked again.

Around me everything was dark. So dark. Hard-to-see dark.

That was right.

Riley and I had gone into the new house where our old house used to stand.

Were we still in the house now?

As my vision began to clear, I spotted Riley in a chair across from me. His head hung down low as if he were still passed out . . . or dead.

A lump formed in my throat.

No, he couldn't be dead. He wouldn't be tied up if he were dead . . . right?

I stared at his chest.

I was almost certain it rose and fell.

He was still alive!

That was definitely something to be thankful for.

My gaze traveled the rest of the space, and I saw the plywood on the walls.

We were definitely at the house Bill was having constructed. In fact, I was in what appeared to be my old living room area right now.

But where was the person who did this?

My gaze fell on something in the corner.

Someone else was in the room.

I startled before realizing who it was.

Sharon.

She lay on a mattress in the corner, her hands and feet bound and a gag over her mouth.

But she appeared to be okay.

That was something else to be thankful for.

However, we were far from being safe. Whoever had done this to us would be back soon. Or maybe he was still here, just lurking out of sight.

Either way, I didn't have time just to sit here and ponder things for too long. I needed to figure out a way to get out of here and to take my friends with me.

I tugged at the ropes behind me again.

Nothing happened. They were tied tightly.

I needed another idea.

I glanced around again, this time looking for something to loosen those ropes.

But there was nothing in this room.

Windows had been placed in the openings, and there was a space cut out where a fire escape was supposed to be, the one that Bill had changed his mind on. Strangely enough, no door or window was there. If I had to guess, contractors had probably ordered it late after Bill had changed his mind.

Since it was open, I wondered if I could scoot toward it, and we could escape somehow that way. But I had a feeling there was nothing on the other side, nothing beneath it.

Falling to my death didn't seem that much better than being killed at the hands of a serial killer.

Think, Gabby. Think.

I looked at Riley again. Why was I awake, but he was still asleep? I would have thought that whatever sedative had been given to us, his would have worn off first.

Another surge of worry filled me.

"Riley," I whispered.

He didn't stir.

I leveraged my feet on the floor and began to hop with my chair toward him. With every motion, I probably only traveled an inch or two. But an inch or two at a time would eventually add up to four or five feet. That was all I needed in order to reach my husband.

I continued scooting, wishing the action didn't require as much energy as it did. But I had to know if Riley was okay.

Finally, I managed to reach him.

Leaning forward in my chair, I said, "Riley?"

He remained still and unmoving.

Worry pulsed through me.

What if he wasn't okay?

Tears pushed their way to the surface.

I couldn't even handle that thought.

Worst-case scenarios played out in my mind. What if this guy had done something horrible to Riley? What if my husband never woke up? What if—

No. Stop it, Gabby. You can't go there.

I needed to focus on the facts. Keep a cool head. Think of solutions.

I studied Riley another moment.

His chest definitely rose and fell.

He was breathing!

Praise God.

Now I just needed to get him to wake up.

I nudged him again, my voice louder this time. "Riley!"

He didn't stir.

But Sharon did.

Her eyes flung open from across the room, and she stared at me. Her temporary fear turned into relief when she spotted me.

She tried to murmur something, but I couldn't understand a word she said because of the gag. For that matter, I was kind of surprised I didn't have a gag. If I yelled loud enough, would somebody hear me outside?

That seemed like a good possibility.

"I'm going to figure out a way to get us out of this," I told Sharon.

She tried to murmur something else while moving frantically.

I still had no idea what she was trying to say.

But right now, I wanted to focus on Riley.

Giving it everything I had, I threw my weight into the chair and rammed into him.

At once, he jostled.

His eyes flung open, and he stared at me.

The next instant, the reality of the situation spread over his features. He slowly closed his eyes, as if wanting to shut out this nightmare.

I couldn't let him slip back into his previous state.

"Stay with me, Riley," I rushed.

He opened his eyes again and glanced around. His face pinched with discomfort before his gaze stopped across the room.

"Sharon?" His voice sounded dry, almost sore.

"I think she's okay."

His gaze met mine again. "Are we in the house still?"

"That's my impression. Are you okay?" I repeated the question because I had to know the answer. I needed to hear it.

He rolled his neck, not looking okay. "Whatever it was we were injected with really knocked me out. I don't even know how long we've been in here."

"Me neither. But it's darker outside than it was earlier."

He rolled his neck again. "It was almost like that guy had some type of blow gun or something, and he shot those darts at us."

That's what I thought also. "The only thing I can figure is that he was in the area where your old apartment used to be. From there, he would have had the right angle. I'm just irritated we didn't hear him beforehand."

"There's no way we could've known. We were being careful."

I glanced at Sharon. Had she seen this guy's face? Could I scoot over to her and pull that gag down? I was sure she knew things that would help us.

But I imagined myself in my chair, trying to reach down to her on the mattress. I didn't see how it would work out. If anything, I'd end up stumbling onto her and hurting her. The chair I was tied to was heavy.

Besides, I needed to say something else to Riley. "There was one person who came to mind right before I passed out."

"Who do you think it is?" Riley's gaze latched onto mine.

I'd had so many theories, all of which had been wrong. I almost hesitated to share my newest theory.

But now that I was ruling certain people out, as well as following my gut, I had a good hunch as to who this might be. I only wished I'd seen it sooner.

"I am pretty sure that the person behind this is—"

Before I could say the man's name out loud, a shadow appeared in the doorway.

It was just who I'd thought it would be.

CHAPTER FORTY-THREE

"I THOUGHT I'D GIVE YOU A FEW MINUTES TO WAKE UP before we had our little rendezvous." The figure stepped into the room, a Glock in his hand.

"Freddy Mansfield." Disgust roiled in my stomach. "I should have known. How didn't I see this from the start?"

As he stepped into a stray beam of light coming from the street outside, he smirked. I halfway expected him to peel back his face, revealing it was in fact a realistic mask. Then Mrs. Mystery would be there or someone else from my past.

But that wasn't the case.

Freddy Mansfield had been the puppet master this whole time.

He continued to smirk. "Easy. You didn't see this

from the start because you're not as smart as you think you are."

"Have I ever claimed to be smart?" Really, I didn't think I had.

His smirk faded slightly. "You don't have to say it with words. Your actions prove it. You always have to keep pushing. Not taking people at their word. Trying to look beyond what's stated."

"That just makes me a decent investigator. Not necessarily the smartest person in the room." I only spoke the truth.

"Obviously."

Now he was just insulting me.

"I wish I could say that I was sorry it had to end this way." Freddy looked anything but sorry with that cold yet curious look in his gaze. "But I'm not. This has been my plan for the past two years. I'm only sorry it took me this long to see everything come to fruition."

"Why would you want to do this, Freddy?" I stared at him as he twirled his gun around his finger, appearing like he didn't have a care in the world. "You've already achieved what you wanted in life. You have a nice but creepy house. You have books out. You've even been featured on national TV programs. Why are you determined to add killer to your list?"

"Because I've spent my whole life studying serial killers!" His voice rose. "The last good one that we had was Milton Jones, and, because of you, he's dead. The world needs someone else to rise up and take his place."

Another cold chill washed over me. "The last thing the world needs is another serial killer."

"Do you know that some serial killers have noble purposes for doing what they're doing? For example, the Green River Killer killed prostitutes because he felt the world was better off without them."

I studied him, hardly wanting to ask my next question. "So what's your purpose?"

He stepped deeper into the room. "I want to keep Milton's memory alive. But I have to do it better than he did. I've planted so many clues along the way that the police are never going to figure this out. Believe me."

I heard the satisfaction in his voice, and the sound of it made me absolutely sick to my stomach.

The next moment, Freddy held up his gun and pointed it at Riley. "There was one more crime I was going to commit before you guys found me. But you beat me. So maybe I'll just do that now."

He grinned as he aimed the barrel at Riley's forehead.

My heart leapt into my throat until I could hardly breathe.

No . . . this couldn't be happening. I had to stop it. Had to think quickly.

"You don't want to do that." The tremble in my voice belied the calm, rational tone I longed for.

"That's where you're wrong. I do want to do this. I really do. It's even better that you're going to be here so I can watch your expression as it happens." His voice was edged with dramatics.

"There are other ways to prove your point." Riley's voice sounded strained.

I could only imagine the thoughts going through his mind. He was probably reliving that terrible, terrible day when his life had been forever changed.

A cry caught in my throat at the thought of it.

"You're the last person I want to talk to." Freddy pulled a rag from his pocket and shoved it into Riley's mouth. Riley fought it but was powerless against Freddy because of his binds. "This is a conversation between Gabby and me."

I stared at his weapon as it was aimed at Riley. I had to try reasoning with this guy. That was the only trick I had up my sleeve right now.

"Everyone's going to hear if you fire a gun," I said. "How does that fit into your plan?"

A moment of doubt flashed in Freddy's eyes. "That's not true. People hear gunfire in this area quite often. They'll probably just think it was fireworks."

"I doubt that. Someone's going to call it in, and the police are going to be here in five minutes flat. If *I* had a plan—"

"There you go trying to be the smartest one in the

room again!" Freddy's voice rose with aggravation. "Why can't you just let me do what I need to do?"

"I'm trying to help you. It doesn't make any sense for you to fire that gun. You haven't come this far just to fail, have you?"

He shifted again until he leered at me. His contempt toward me practically dripped from his eyes. "Maybe I should just shoot you so I can shut you up. It seems like I have some decisions to make."

Cement hardened my lungs as I waited to see what he would do next. I was all out of ideas on how to stop him.

At least, for the moment.

But I wasn't done fighting.

Not by any means.

Squeaky Clean is the best. All the others won't pass the test.

I *was* Squeaky Clean. It was in my blood. My history. Maybe my future.

And now I needed to prove I was the best.

"You think I don't have a plan, but I do." Freddy stared at me. Still holding his gun. Still looking at me with contempt. Still trying to prove he was the smartest person in the room.

"What exactly is your plan?" I stared him in the eye,

not allowing myself to give him the satisfaction of looking away.

Clarice's jingle still echoed in my head. *And we do it all with zest.*

Zest, Gabby. Think zest.

"The truth is, I thought shooting you would be boring." Freddy's head wobbled as he said the words, as if his thoughts were so big that he could hardly contain them. "So expected. Overdone. Really a coward's way out because it's so easy for a person just to pull a trigger and then run."

"So what did you decide?" Part of me didn't want to know, but the good news was I was buying time.

Not that we had anyone looking for us.

But maybe I could think of something in the interim.

"I remembered your first case with that fire." Freddy glanced around the room as if imagining something horrifically wonderful—in his mind, at least. "I thought maybe I could set this place on fire. That would seem rather poetic."

A fire wasn't at the top of my list of ways I wouldn't mind dying.

I needed to buy more time, to keep him talking before he did something rash. "You set that first crime scene on fire, didn't you? The one Clarice and I were working at Regina Black's place."

That got a smile out of Freddy. "I did. I heard about the crime, so I planted that gun after the police left.

Then I left a Squeaky Clean card with the woman's son and kept my fingers crossed that he'd be calling you. I keep tabs on you. When I heard you'd been called, I set my plan in action from there."

"Aren't you clever?" And by clever I meant dastardly and evil.

"I *knew* my plan was going to be perfect. And it was. You found that gun, and, as soon as you did, I set the front of that house on fire. I figured you guys would get out in time. But it was still thrilling for me." Delight raced through his gaze, and he looked like a newly minted hunter who'd gotten his first kill.

"Then you did the same at the next scene?"

"It's amazing what you can learn by using a police scanner and doing a little research."

"Did you purposefully dress in that Georgetown sweatshirt when you talked to that kid about leaving the package at our door?" I already knew his answer, but I wanted to hear it with my own ears.

"The best way to make *you* suffer is to make those you love suffer." Freddy said the words casually, as if simply talking about the weather. "Riley and I are about the same height, and we both have dark hair. It really wasn't that hard to pull off. It was one more way of messing with your head—which, I must say, is *such* a delight."

"The songs were a nice touch. How did you know I liked music so much?"

"Weren't they a great touch? I even thought about recording one of your ridiculous jingle ideas."

My blood felt a little colder. "How did you know about those?"

"You used to talk about them to people. Quite gregarious, you are sometimes. Not always. You're a complexity of outgoing and introvert, of off the wall and yet on the nose, focused but flighty."

I shrugged. "What can I say? I like to keep people on their toes."

I glanced around, trying to figure out Freddy's next step, to slip into his mind for a moment and somehow jump a few steps ahead. "I suppose you've ultimately decided not to kill us by fire. That wouldn't be dramatic enough."

"That's right. I want to do something more creative, something that can serve as my signature. That's why I thought about suffocating you. It's still a possibility."

I couldn't let my thoughts go there. I needed to keep him talking instead. "Did you kill the man who was found in the attic? I know all about his connection to the family currently living in the Cunningham's old house."

"I did. I wondered if you'd realize the connection between him and your first case. I left another card for the family of the man who died in that house too, knowing you'd probably be called there." He paused for just a moment. "Some of my actions were risky. I couldn't guarantee that you were going to be the one there. But I figured I'd have to play some of those cases by ear. To my delight, the first two worked out so well for me. Did that clean-up job bring back a lot of memories, Gabby?"

I really despised this man. So much. So, so much. "The whole thing definitely brought back memories. Memories of how I ended up tracking the bad guy down and how justice was finally served."

I probably shouldn't have gone there. Freddy narrowed his eyes.

That statement hadn't made him happy, and I should have known better. After all, I didn't want to trigger this man.

He paced in front of me, still holding his gun. "That's when I remembered my favorite case that you solved. It's all out of order, don't get me wrong. That wasn't ideal, but sometimes, you have to veer off your original plan, just for the thrill of it."

I swallowed hard. "And what case is that?"

"The death of Emma Jean McCormick."

I sucked in a quick breath. "Bill's wife?"

Freddy nodded, a smile tugging at his lips. "Death by poisoning? Oleander? Politics? I mean, that whole case could have been a movie. It was fascinating."

"That's why you sent me the song that included the line about sleepy Jean." I shook my head. "I should have known. But I thought it was Bill giving me a hint that it was him."

Based on the smile on his face, Freddy found satisfaction in my words. "That's right. Poisoning. Actually, I thought it could be fun to do a combination. Maybe I can poison you *then* set this place on fire. That would cover up most of the clues. Isn't that a brilliant idea?"

Brilliant? Maybe.

But it was an evil kind of brilliant that made me sick to my stomach.

CHAPTER FORTY-FOUR

"I'm going to go down in history books," Freddy continued. "I'm not going to fit the typical pattern of serial killers. Police aren't going to be able to pinpoint my MO exactly. And that's going to allow me to get away with this for a long time."

"But if you don't have a pattern, how are the authorities going to connect your cases?"

"That's the point." His voice rose again. "It's going to take them a long time, and that's going to make me look even smarter than I look now."

"You're essentially going to be leading them astray by framing other people?"

"Exactly!"

"But most serial killers want to be famous, not hide. You're framing other people."

Yes, I was trying to get him frazzled. He'd already started pacing, and I could tell my efforts to mess with his head were working. That was exactly what I wanted.

"You don't understand anything at all!" His voice continued to rise.

"I'm trying to help you." I kept my expression placid, knowing I needed him to believe my words.

"Because you're so smart?" Bitterness dripped from his voice.

"No, because you set up this elaborate plan. You don't want to disappoint people, do you?"

He was silent for a moment before chuckling. "You and I are more alike than you want to admit."

I didn't know about that. But I wasn't going to argue with him on that point right now. Maybe if he felt like we had some commonality that would help us in the long run.

I swallowed hard before asking, "What are you going to do after you finish us off?"

"I haven't decided yet. But I'll find a new victim. Several of them. And I'll study them. I'll learn their routines. Then I'll find a crime fitting of their death."

I repressed a shudder. This man was sick. He knew it, and he didn't care. He'd been obsessed with serial killers for so long that the next logical step for him had been becoming a serial killer himself.

I stared at that opening behind him—the one where

the fire escape would have been. It was dark outside, and the cutout nearly blended in with the pitch blackness outside.

That's when the first niggle of a plan appeared in my head.

It was a long shot, but my idea just might work.

I licked my lips before saying, "You could leave a bomb. A bomb is effective."

"I know, right? It makes such a bang." He chuckled at himself. "Get it. Bang?"

I ignored his attempt at humor. "I can see it now. Someone getting a box on the front step. They'll think it's a present. Just like the one that you sent me. But then they open it and . . ." My eyes widened.

"That's right. They see it and then *boom*." He took a step back, a step closer to that opening.

How could I get him to take just a couple more steps in that direction?

I had to think, and I had to think quickly.

He seemed quite content to act out some of his crimes in front of me. What kind of crime would involve him scooting backward?

Or was I being naïve to think that this could work?

I didn't know.

But this plan was the only thing I had right now.

"That's right," I started. "They're going to see that package. Then the next person you decide to focus on is going to see a package, and they're going to feel a shot of fear, whether it's a bomb or not. Just like what happened with me."

"That's right. Fear is a good thing." Satisfaction lit his gaze.

"So, as I see it, your victim is going to back away, afraid to make any wrong move."

"That's right." He had an expression of stark fear on his face as he raised his hands and took a step back.

I held my breath.

Just as I hoped, his foot stepped off the platform.

His arms flailed in the air.

As he did, his index finger must have jerked.

A gunshot split the air.

I held my breath, praying the bullet hadn't hit anybody.

The next instant, Freddy fell from the second story.

I held my breath as I heard him scream.

Then I heard the sickening sound of someone hitting the ground.

Now my question was . . . had he survived?

It took only ten minutes for the police to arrive.

Detective Adams was one of the cops on the scene.

His eyes widened when he saw us. The next instant, he cut the ropes from my wrists and ankles.

He did the same for Riley and took his gag out as well.

Paramedics rushed into the room to assist Sharon.

As they whisked her way, she mouthed "thank you" to me. I knew we'd have time to catch up later.

But right now, there was only one question on my mind. "Is Freddy dead?"

Adams nodded. "We found his body outside. I need to get a statement from you about what happened."

Relief pulsed through me. The next instant, I rushed toward Riley. I wrapped my arms around him, praying I never had to let him go.

My future was with this man. I wanted to have babies with him. Have a family. Have a normal, albeit nosy, life.

"How did you know we were here?" I asked Adams, still not letting go of Riley.

"Neighbors reported the gunshot and the scream."

I knew it. Even in crime-ridden areas, neighbors still liked to watch out for each other. I knew somebody would want to help.

"Are you two ready to give your statements?" Adams asked. "I can have the paramedics check you out."

I touched my neck, which still tender from where that dart had hit me. Otherwise, I felt fine physically. "I think I'm okay."

Detective Adams glanced to me again before slowly

nodding. "Okay then. I need to hear what happened. All of it."

I slipped my hand into Riley's.

It appeared that this was all finally over.

Praise the Lord.

CHAPTER FORTY-FIVE

I GRINNED AS MY DAD AND TEDDI KISSED AFTER PASTOR Shaggy pronounced them husband and wife.

They'd finally done it. They were married.

I paused for a moment and surveyed from the stage everyone who'd come to share the big day with them. I was surprised by how many familiar faces were here.

That's when I realized that most of my friends had also become my dad and Teddi's friends.

For starters, Tim was here. He'd gotten out of jail and had gone to live at my dad's place. He seemed sober and had told me before the ceremony that he wasn't going to mess up again.

I wanted to believe him. I really did. And I hoped he told the truth.

Trace Ryan, my new stepbrother, was here. He even sang a special song during the ceremony. He'd be performing a few more numbers at the reception, which would take place in the courtyard outside the historic church building.

He was doing really well, and it was great to see him.

All my friends were there, including Sierra and Chad, Clarice and Sharon, and Bill and his new girl-friend. Garrett had come with a date. Even Parker had shown up—solo. Maybe being single would be good for him.

I could rest easy knowing that Freddy would no longer hurt anyone. Milton Jones was really dead. And justice had been served.

I only wished that so many people hadn't gotten hurt in the process.

After the recessional—"I Will Always Love You," Dolly Parton version—we all met outside. String lights had been set up, the air was perfectly crisp, and the scent of mini frankfurters in barbeque sauce and grape-glazed meatballs filled the air.

Riley found me and kissed my cheek. "That dress is so . . ."

"Sexy?"

"That wasn't the word I was going to use. If you were ever in a play featuring angels and demons—"

"I could play a demon." I nodded and patted one of my spiky sleeves. "I get it."

Riley grinned before looking back at the mingling crowds. "The ceremony was nice."

"Wasn't it? I'm really happy for Dad. This has been a long time coming." Though no one could ever replace my mom, I was glad my dad had the chance to rewrite his story.

"We all deserve second chances."

I nodded slowly, thinking about my own life and all the mistakes I'd made. "Yes, we definitely do."

Someone touched my elbow, and I turned to see Chad and Sierra standing there. I threw my arms around my best friend's neck. It didn't matter that I'd seen her multiple times since she was released from jail. I was so glad she was okay—and her baby.

"That was so beautiful," Sierra said. "I never thought I'd really see this day."

"I'm so glad you could be here." The police had found receipts proving that Freddy was behind that bombing. Sierra had been cleared.

Chad scooted closer. "I just wanted to say again that I'm really sorry about how I acted after Sierra was arrested. I shouldn't have blamed you."

"It's okay. I know you were upset." I really did understand. He was only trying to protect the people he loved.

Chad wrapped his arm around Sierra's waist. "You've been a great friend to us throughout the years,

Gabby. You're one of my best friends, for that matter. I'm sorry for everything you've been through."

"There's one way you can make it up to me."

Chad raised an eyebrow. "What's that?"

"You can use the jingle Clarice and I came up with for your company. 'Squeaky Clean is the best—'"

He raised his hand. "If only I had money in the budget."

We all laughed at his obvious sarcasm.

Before I could continue to give Chad a hard time, I spotted someone across the crowd and excused myself. I made my way toward Sharon and Clarice.

Sharon looked good, especially considering everything that had happened. I could still see a few small bruises on her face, and her gaze looked different. Trauma could do that.

But she had a fighting spirt, and I'd made it my goal to check on her every day.

"I'm so glad you made it," I told her.

She raised a glass of punch. "I'm honored I was invited."

I touched her arm, not wanting to pretend like everything was normal when it wasn't. "How are you today?"

Her gaze dipped as she shrugged. "I still have nightmares."

"I know." I frowned, wishing I could take all the pain away. But that was impossible. All I could do was be there for her. "I'm so sorry you went through what you did."

"I don't blame you, Gabby. Freddy was a very sick man. I'm just glad it's all over."

"Aunt Sharon, let's go try the chocolate fountain." Clarice joined us. "What do you think? My mouth is watering right now."

Sharon smiled. "Let's go—strawberries are my favorite."

When I joined Riley again, I saw Parker had joined the circle.

He looked me up and down as I stepped closer. "Nice dress."

I frowned. How many times would I have to hear that?

I offered a little curtsy. "Thank you."

Parker shifted. "Listen, in case I didn't tell you, Gabby, good job with the case. Thanks to you, an evil man is off the streets."

"If I'd figured it out about three hours earlier, it would have been even better." I shrugged. "But thank you."

He took something from his pocket and placed it in my hand. I glanced down. It was a business card for someone named Sheila Stewart.

"What's this?"

"I have a friend who's an independent forensic

anthropologist. She's been looking for an assistant. I told her about you."

"Don't you have to have a medical degree for this?"

He shrugged. "You study graves as well as bodies. I don't know everything that's involved. But you should call her. I could see your skill set working in this kind of job. After all, you've been examining the dead for a long time—every time you've cleaned a crime scene."

I handed the card to Riley. "Hold onto this for me, please."

Unfortunately, my dress had no pockets. His suit did.

"Will do," Riley said.

Maybe I would contact Sheila. I'd been praying for direction. Had it ultimately come from my ex?

How . . . unexpected, to say the least.

Mostly, I was excited about the possibilities for the future. The winds of change were blowing, as the saying went.

Riley turned to me. "What are you thinking?"

"You really want to know?"

"Of course."

I raised my jazz hands. "If you've been shot, if you've been stabbed, if blood on your walls says, 'Someone's been bad,' Gabby Thomas is the-e-re for you."

Riley grinned and shook his head. "Really?"

"I think I'll put that on my résumé."

He hooked his arm around my neck and pulled me

close enough to plant a kiss on my forehead. "You are one of a kind, Gabby. And I love that about you. I absolutely love it."

As Trace began singing in the background, I put my arms around Riley's neck and we swayed back and forth to a song Trace had written about freezing time.

I wished I could freeze this moment.

I couldn't.

But I'd always remember the wedding as a reunion of sorts.

And I'd try to forget the gruesome walk down memory lane I'd just experienced.

New beginnings were in sight . . . and I couldn't wait to see what the future had in store.

COMPLETE BOOK LIST

#14 Cold Case: Clean Sweep

#15 Cold Case: Clean Break

#16 Cleans to an End (coming soon)

While You Were Sweeping, A Riley Thomas Spinoff

The Sierra Files:

#1 Pounced

#2 Hunted

#3 Pranced

#4 Rattled

The Gabby St. Claire Diaries (a Tween Mystery series):

The Curtain Call Caper

The Disappearing Dog Dilemma

The Bungled Bike Burglaries

The Worst Detective Ever

#1 Ready to Fumble

#2 Reign of Error

#3 Safety in Blunders

#4 Join the Flub

#5 Blooper Freak

#6 Flaw Abiding Citizen

#7 Gaffe Out Loud

#8 Joke and Dagger

#9 Wreck the Halls

#10 Glitch and Famous (coming soon)

Raven Remington

Relentless 1

Relentless 2 (coming soon)

Holly Anna Paladin Mysteries:

#1 Random Acts of Murder

#2 Random Acts of Deceit

#2.5 Random Acts of Scrooge

#3 Random Acts of Malice

#4 Random Acts of Greed

#5 Random Acts of Fraud

#6 Random Acts of Outrage

#7 Random Acts of Iniquity

Lantern Beach Mysteries

#1 Hidden Currents

#2 Flood Watch

#3 Storm Surge

#4 Dangerous Waters

#5 Perilous Riptide

#6 Deadly Undertow

Lantern Beach Romantic Suspense

Tides of Deception

Shadow of Intrigue

Storm of Doubt

Winds of Danger

Rains of Remorse

Torrents of Fear

Lantern Beach P.D.
On the Lookout
Attempt to Locate
First Degree Murder
Dead on Arrival
Plan of Action

Lantern Beach Escape
Afterglow (a novelette)

Lantern Beach Blackout
Dark Water
Safe Harbor
Ripple Effect
Rising Tide

Crime á la Mode
Deadman's Float
Milkshake Up
Bomb Pop Threat
Banana Split Personalities

The Sidekick's Survival Guide
The Art of Eavesdropping
The Perks of Meddling
The Exercise of Interfering

The Practice of Prying

The Skill of Snooping

The Craft of Being Covert

Saltwater Cowboys

Saltwater Cowboy

Breakwater Protector

Cape Corral Keeper

Seagrass Secrets

Driftwood Danger

Carolina Moon Series

Home Before Dark

Gone By Dark

Wait Until Dark

Light the Dark

Taken By Dark

Suburban Sleuth Mysteries:

Death of the Couch Potato's Wife

Fog Lake Suspense:

Edge of Peril

Margin of Error

Brink of Danger

Line of Duty

Cape Thomas Series:

Dubiosity
Disillusioned
Distorted

Standalone Romantic Mystery:
The Good Girl

Suspense:
Imperfect
The Wrecking

Sweet Christmas Novella:
Home to Chestnut Grove

Standalone Romantic-Suspense:
Keeping Guard
The Last Target
Race Against Time
Ricochet
Key Witness
Lifeline
High-Stakes Holiday Reunion
Desperate Measures
Hidden Agenda
Mountain Hideaway
Dark Harbor
Shadow of Suspicion
The Baby Assignment

The Cradle Conspiracy

Trained to Defend

Mountain Survival (coming soon)

Nonfiction:

Characters in the Kitchen

Changed: True Stories of Finding God through Christian Music (out of print)

The Novel in Me: The Beginner's Guide to Writing and Publishing a Novel (out of print)

ABOUT THE AUTHOR

USA Today has called Christy Barritt's books "scary, funny, passionate, and quirky."

Christy writes both mystery and romantic suspense novels that are clean with underlying messages of faith. Her books have won the Daphne du Maurier Award for Excellence in Suspense and Mystery, have been twice nominated for the Romantic Times Reviewers' Choice Award, and have finaled for both a Carol Award and Foreword Magazine's Book of the Year.

She is married to her Prince Charming, a man who thinks she's hilarious—but only when she's not trying to be. Christy is a self-proclaimed klutz, an avid music lover who's known for spontaneously bursting into song, and a road trip aficionado.

When she's not working or spending time with her family, she enjoys singing, playing the guitar, and exploring small, unsuspecting towns where people have no idea how accident-prone she is.

Find Christy online at:

www.christybarritt.com
www.facebook.com/christybarritt
www.twitter.com/cbarritt

Sign up for Christy's newsletter to get information on all of her latest releases here: **www.christybarritt.com/ newsletter-sign-up/**

If you enjoyed this book, please consider leaving a review.

Made in the USA
Las Vegas, NV
22 April 2024

89027273R00187